48

HOURS

To Kenneth, the Inspirationist's
Inspiration!

First American Edition 2019
Kane Miller, A Division of EDC Publishing

Text copyright © Gabrielle Lord, 2017.
Illustration and design copyright © Scholastic Australia, 2017.
Cover illustration by Ben Jelfs, Redrum Studios.

First published by Scholastic Australia Pty Limited in 2017.
This edition published under license from Scholastic Australia Pty Limited.

Additional illustrations: 404 © istockphoto.com/zentilia; abstract overlay © istockphoto.com/Godruma; boy
© shutterstock.com/MJTH; DNA © istockphoto.com/Firstsignal; emoticon © istockphoto.com/Pingebat;
engineer © istockphoto.com/Georgijevic; flare © shutterstock.com/pixelparticle; footprints © shutterstock.
com/Jason Winter; hair © istockphoto.com/Firstsignal; hexagons © istockphoto.com/tonivaver; nails
© istockphoto.com/BackyardProduction; pixels © istockphoto.com/dikobraziy; rust © istockphoto.
com/Ludibarrs; sand © shutterstock.com/Michael Milvich; SUV © istockphoto.com/Skyak; woman ©
istockphoto.com/aldomurillo; wood © istockphoto.com/germi_p.

For information contact:
Kane Miller, A Division of EDC Publishing
PO Box 470663
Tulsa, OK 74147-0663
www.kanemiller.com
www.usbornebooksandmore.com
www.edcpub.com

Library of Congress Control Number: 2018958283
Printed and bound in the United States of America
1 2 3 4 5 6 7 8 9 10
ISBN: 978-1-61067-865-0

GABRIELLE LORD

48
HOURS
THE VANISHING

Kane Miller
A DIVISION OF EDC PUBLISHING

CODE 7-0!
ROBBERY IN PROGRESS!

"**C**ode 7-0, repeat Code 7-0! Robbery in progress!" Detective Jazmine Mandell yelled back to base through her lapel mike as she dashed across the street. Her notebook and pen were already in one hand, the other releasing the catch on her holster in case she needed to draw her gun. "Robbery in progress!"

A black car screeched away from the curb in front of a shop, broken glass crunching under its tires. "Plate check requested," Jazmine called into the lapel mike, quickly reading out the license plate on the getaway car.

As much as she wanted to jump in a squad car and speed after the burglars, catching criminals was always a team effort. As a patrol car's sirens blared in the distance, Jazmine turned and ran to assist the slumped figure of the shop owner, who lay crumpled and bleeding among the smashed glass of his front display window.

"Request backup and ambulance!" she ordered into her mike.

Expensive watches and necklaces were scattered all over the sidewalk. The thieves had dropped the goods in their rush to escape.

Jazmine turned to her partner. "Sergeant, make sure there's no one else inside. Remember to tread carefully. We don't want to lose any physical evidence!" She lowered her voice, nodding toward the sniffling shop owner. "I think this witness needs some space."

Slowly, she squatted beside the injured man and placed a comforting hand on his shoulder. "It'll be OK," she said. "Just take your time. When you're ready I'll get a statement from you."

A police car pulled up. Detective Jazmine Mandell stood and saluted the chief inspector as she stepped out of the car. "I've got the license plate," Jazmine reported. "Whoever this gang of burglars is, we're going to catch them soon."

"I don't doubt it, Mandell," said the chief inspector. "Not with you on the case."

THE UNSOLVED CRIME

"Thank you, Chief," Jazmine murmured to herself as she walked along a tree-lined street on her way to school. She tucked a stray lock of thick blonde hair behind her ear.

"Earth to Jazmine, hello?"

"Huh?" Jazmine snapped out of her daydream and turned to find her friend Mackenzie glaring at her through narrowed dark eyes.

"Aside from that mumbling, you haven't said a word since we started walking to Anika's!" Mackenzie fumed, flinging her loose, long black hair over her shoulder in a huff. "Jazz, it's bad enough with Anika going on about that old journal she found, and now you won't even talk to me because you're busy solving crimes in your head. Plus you nearly walked into that tree!"

"Sorry, Mack," said Jazz. "I promise to talk to you the whole way to Anika's, and then I'll even talk to both of you the rest of the way to school." Taller than nearly all the other girls in her class, Jazz could almost rest her chin on her friend's head as she gave Mack's shoulders a friendly squeeze.

"Welcome back," said Mack drily. "So, have you been studying for today's math test?"

"All you want to talk about is studying! You know, I read in *Victims and How to Identify Them* that people who are obsessed with work or study are far more likely to be the victims of crime." Jazz sounded frustrated, but her sideways grin told Mack she was joking.

"Be serious, Jazz. Don't you care about your marks?" Mack asked.

"All I care about is beating Phoenix Lyons, and since he got suspended I don't have to worry about that!"

"True, and at least now I'm top of computer class." Mack grinned. Then she hunched her shoulders and said quietly, "If we're talking obsession, it's Anika and her blog of that journal we should be worried about."

"I know," grimaced Jazz.

"I thought it would be right up your alley," Mack teased, nudging Jazz with her elbow. "Doesn't Anika say it holds the secrets to some great unsolved crime?

Come on, Detective Mandell, what do *you* think happened to the woman in the journal?"

"How should I know?" snapped Jazz, moving her arm away from Mack, irritated. "I'm not reading Anika's blog. I'm her best friend! I shouldn't have to find out with everyone else. Why can't she just tell us about it?"

Mack sighed. "You two aren't going to fight about it all the way to school, are you? I need to concentrate on memorizing formulas for our math test."

"Do you reckon you could take the grade fixation down a notch or two, Mack?" teased Jazz, happy to be changing the topic. Jazz made waving hand motions around Mackenzie's head and chanted, "You are worthy, regardless of your test scores."

"Try telling my parents that," scowled Mack. Where Jazz dreamed of becoming a famous detective, Mack dreamed of doing the best she could on all her exams to make her parents proud. Dr. Zhang, her dad, was under lots of pressure to make the museum he managed profitable, and her mum was busy with Mack's younger brother. Mack didn't want to cause them any more trouble.

Jazz suddenly grabbed Mack's arm and hurried her along. "Hey!" cried Mack. "What are you doing?"

"Shh," whispered Jazz urgently. "That's where

Phoenix lives. I don't want him to see us walking past!"

Once safely out of sight of the house, Jazz asked, "Do you know what he did to get suspended?"

"It was a denial-of-service attack on the school's servers. Apparently they won't let him come back till he writes a letter of apology."

Jazz detected a hint of admiration in Mack's voice. "Well, I hope he's not spending the whole time studying so he can get ahead."

"I doubt it," said Mack. "He's probably messing around in his mum's forensics lab looking at computer parts under a microscope or something."

Turning into Anika's street, Jazz and Mack walked past the overgrown gardens of the gloomy mansion "Deepwater" that stood next to the Belmonts' house. Jazz blinked as she glanced at the upper windows. "Hey, did you see something up there? A tiny glint of light?"

Mack just looked at Jazz. "Really? Now you're making up ghost stories about that place too?"

Jazz often told Mack about how she and Anika had played in the grounds of the once-grand house when they were kids. The building had been fenced off long ago, and now security patrolled it regularly. Earlier in the year, Anika had written and published a ghost story on her blog, set in the decaying mansion, which had attracted a lot of online followers.

"Actually, if I remember it right, you're plagiarizing," Mack said. "Didn't Anika's story say, 'From an upper window in Deepwater—the derelict mansion which, despite its decay, still loomed over the street—someone was watching; the glint of light on binoculars the only clue that someone lurked inside the uninhabitable mansion'?" Mack quoted in a deep, spooky voice.

"Fine, I must have been seeing things," Jazz pouted.

Arriving at Anika's, they ran through the half-opened gate of the elegant house and along the walkway, then up the three steps to the shady front porch. Jazz pulled out her key to the Belmonts' house. Anika's parents left early for their jobs in the city, but were strict about keeping the house secure. They had allowed Anika to give Jazz a spare key so she could let herself in while Anika kept getting ready.

Jazz unlocked the heavy front door and she and Mack went inside. They clattered up the stairs to Anika's bedroom.

Anika was sitting on the rug, her runner's legs stretched out in front of her as she tapped away at her laptop. The journal lay open on the floorboards. "I've just got a few more lines to type," she said.

"Hurry *up*," said Mack. "I don't want to be late!"

"Would you just chill out?" said Anika. "I'm on to something huge here. Tonight I'll reveal the final journal entry and then the world can try to solve the mystery!"

"I could have solved it if you'd just let me read it," sulked Jazz.

"But, hello, you can. I'm blogging it! One entry at a time. You know what you're like. If I gave you the advantage of reading it first, you'd be at school in some daydream and end up just blabbing it out loud. It wouldn't be fair to all the other readers waiting so *patiently* to unlock the clues themselves!"

"Yeah, right. It's no big deal anyway when your whole audience is just people from school," Jazz said.

"That's not true. There are other people who read it," said Anika, sounding hurt. "They leave comments. You can tell they're not schoolkids. And they're really hooked. I know you're dying to read it, Jazz."

Jazz didn't want to admit how right Anika was. It was too late to back down now. "If you won't let me read the whole thing, I don't want to read it at all!"

"Suit yourself, Jazz." Anika snapped her laptop shut and put it back on her desk, along with the journal. She scooped her glossy brown hair up into a high ponytail and grabbed her schoolbag. Just before she stormed out the door, she turned and said, "But it's your loss!"

THE FIRST 48 HOURS

Jazz paused as she came in her front door after school. In preparation for becoming a detective, she liked to test her observation skills every day, and knew better than to barge in and disturb any potential evidence or clues, even in her own house.

She crossed her arms and drummed her fingers, her habit when she was thinking. First she checked the shoes and jackets by the front door. As expected, her mum's work shoes were missing from the rack, but her grocery bag stash was also missing. "I deduce she's gone to work, followed by grocery shopping," muttered Jazz. "Yay, no leftovers tonight!"

Heading into the kitchen, Jazz immediately noticed the smell of toast and several dirty dishes in the sink. "Tim must have an assignment due," she said to herself.

"But which subject is it for?" she wondered.

Jazz's keen observations had shown there was a pattern to her older brother's study snacking. She pulled out her tablet and opened up CrimeSeen, an app that let you track all the evidence in an investigation. She'd been hoping to use it for real detective work, but for now she clicked through to the chart headed Snacks vs. Subjects.

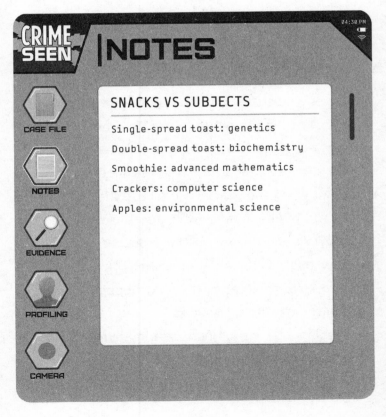

CRIME SEEN | NOTES
04:30 PM

CASE FILE
NOTES
EVIDENCE
PROFILING
CAMERA

SNACKS VS SUBJECTS

Single-spread toast: genetics
Double-spread toast: biochemistry
Smoothie: advanced mathematics
Crackers: computer science
Apples: environmental science

Jazz examined the knives in the sink and detected traces of both jam *and* peanut butter. "Double-spread toast," she murmured, "is consistent with study for . . . biochemistry."

Happy with her deductions, she pulled her latest true crime book out of her bag: *Crimes that Stopped the Nation.* She settled onto the couch and started to read.

> The efficient gathering of evidence has been vital to solving many of the nation's most shocking crimes. When investigating a crime scene, the effective investigator always remembers two things: it is important to be careful, and to take the time to find all the required evidence. Investigators must also keep their eye on the clock, however. The first **48 HOURS** after a crime has been committed are vital to collecting the freshest and most useful evidence.

"Interesting," Jazz mused, as she grabbed a highlighter and colored over "The first **48 HOURS**," then underlined it several times.

She turned to her phone and checked her Facebook feed. Jazz smiled when she saw Mack's picture of her grinning little brother, covered ear to ear in broccoli. She "liked" it, and then saw Anika had already left a comment: "Too cute!!!" Jazz's stomach twisted uncomfortably. Normally the three of them would be chatting online right now. Jazz and Anika had been best friends since kindergarten, sharing all their secrets and vacationing together. They'd met Mack at the start of high school, and the trio had become inseparable since, constantly talking on the phone or messaging. But since their fight this morning, Anika had ignored her, and Jazz couldn't bring herself to apologize. Especially as ever since Anika had started blogging this journal she seemed to have time for nothing else, not even her best friends.

Jazz found herself clicking on Anika's profile. She scrolled to the very first post about the journal.

Anika Belmont
A few months ago · 🌐

OMG just found the most amazing thing! I was stretching after a run and I overbalanced and knocked into this old mirror that's been on my wall since like forever, even before we moved in. I totally crashed to the ground and thought "Mum is gonna be so mad" because she thinks the mirror's worth loads, but then something hit me on the head! It was a journal that had been hidden behind the mirror! I started reading it and OMG! It's all about this terrible crime that probably happened in this very room. I'm going to blog it every day. Read all about it here!!!

👍 Like   💬 Comment   ➔ Share

😮 32   8 Comments   13 Shares

Write a comment…

Jazz felt angry all over again. If Anika wanted to solve the mystery, she should have given the journal to *her*—she was the crime expert—not put it up there for everyone to read. Scrolling through her feed again, a new post came up from Anika.

Jazz threw her phone down, trying to ignore how much she wanted to click on the link and read the whole story. "Stupid blog," she muttered. She was relieved to be distracted by the sound of her mother coming in the front door.

"Jazz, are you home?" called Mrs. Mandell. "Can you help with these groceries?"

Jazz jumped up and ran to the car to lift out the rest of the bags. She knew how important it was that she and Tim did as much around the house as they could. It had just been the three of them for a long time, and for the last four years that Jazz had been in high school her mum had gone back to full-time work as an office manager.

"How was school today?" her mum asked as they started unpacking.

"Pretty good," said Jazz. "The math test was hard but I reckon I did OK. Mack was pretty stressed about it."

"And Anika?" Mrs. Mandell asked. When Jazz didn't reply she continued, "You haven't said much about her lately. Everything OK?"

Jazz hadn't told her mum that she and Anika were fighting, but she should have known Mum would pick up that something wasn't right.

"She won't let me help with a project that I'd be really good at," complained Jazz.

"Well," said her mum thoughtfully, "give her a chance and maybe she'll ask for help when she needs it."

"It'll be too late by then!" Jazz huffed.

Jazz put the last of the groceries away, then got out some vegetables for dinner. While she cut up the veggies she could forget about being mad at Anika. Or at least take it out on the chopping board for a little while. *Slice. Slice. SLICE!*

* * *

All through dinner Anika was impatient to get back up to her room to see what comments people had left on her latest blog post. Finally, the table was cleared and she was free. She raced back upstairs to her laptop.

Anika smiled when she saw plenty of likes already popping up on her Facebook feed. She was so keen to see what her friends thought now that the whole story was online, and she wanted to check if Jazz's name was among them, but a new notification caught her eye—a comment! She frowned, though, as she read it, her happy mood collapsing:

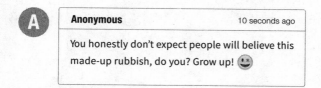

Anika wondered fleetingly if the anonymous hostile comment could be from Jazz, but then shook her head, dismissing the thought. They might be fighting, but Jazz would never be that mean.

Her last thoughts as she drifted off to sleep later that night were to hope that soon she could convince Jazz to read the whole blog. Then they could go back to being friends, and maybe even track down the truth about the mystery woman's identity together.

48:0

0:00

47:46

Anika jolted awake. It was still dark. She lay listening, puzzled. She could hear a soft whirring sound. It sounded a bit like her mum's electric toothbrush, but why would she be brushing her teeth in the middle of the night?

"Mum?" Anika groggily called out. "What time is it?"

No one answered. She blinked at the alarm clock . . . **12:14 AM**.

The noise stopped. *Maybe I imagined it*, she thought. A dream had probably woken her up.

But then the whirring started again. This was no dream. Anika strained her ears to work out where the noise was coming from. It sounded like it was coming from . . . *inside* the wall. Could it be? Was it a rat? But rats didn't use electric toothbrushes, at any time of night.

The noise stopped again. Anika held her breath, still listening hard. Just as she started to exhale and think about sleep she heard a thud.

This time she sat bolt upright, her heart beating faster.

Anika stared into the darkness. There was a crack and a creak, and suddenly an eerie line of light became visible on the wall. The wall was moving! Anika sat rigid with shock, her throat paralyzed, as a whole panel of wall moved away and a silhouetted figure emerged.

Then she heard something else. A swishing sound snaked through the still air of her room, whispering her name.

"Anikaaaa."

What was happening? Her parents' bedroom was at the other end of the hallway. But if she screamed loud enough, maybe they'd hear her. The second she thought this, the whisperer hissed.

"Don't scream or you'll be sorry!"

The figure loomed closer.

"If you scream," it continued, "I promise you'll make everything so much worse." It wasn't the words but the horror that held Anika's tongue. Walking across the room was an unbelievable figure, humanoid but not human. It lumbered on gargantuan legs, a grotesquely large head atop its hulking form. Its voice was like something from another planet.

"Don't make a sound and everything will be all right, Anika. Listen carefully. I want the journal and the box. Get up, and give them to me!"

This isn't happening. This can't be happening, she told herself.

Her fear kicked in fully and she took in a deep breath to scream, but the figure loomed even closer.

"Let's do this the easy way. The journal and the box," it hissed. "Give them to me and I'll go away."

The menacing voice chilled Anika. The figure stepped back as, trembling, she slowly got out of bed. The creature watched as she went to her desk and picked up the thick journal, the red-and-white cover appearing gray in the ghostly light.

"The box," it hissed. "Where's the wooden jewelry box?"

Anika could only whimper, "I only read about it; I don't know where it is. Just take the journal!"

"I need the box, the journal is only half the story," hissed the monster. Anika watched in petrified silence as the monster shone its flashlight around her room, searching in drawers, the bookcase, her closet. It turned back to the bed and shone the bright light into Anika's face.

"Lasssst chance. Tell me where the box is."

"I don't know," sobbed Anika.

The intruder seemed to think for a moment. "Then you'll have to come with me."

Suddenly the invader lunged at her and Anika felt a sharp sting in the side of her neck. The last thing Anika noticed was the sense of falling . . .

falling . . .

falling . . .

40:00

"**W**hat did you put for question three on the math test yesterday?" Mack asked Jazz while they walked along the leafy street to Anika's place, as the friends did every school morning.

"Mack, I don't have a photographic memory of the test!" laughed Jazz. Mack's phone pinged. "That's the sixth notification you've had this morning," said Jazz, raising her eyebrows. "How come you're so popular?"

Mack looked a little sheepish. "Actually, it's comments coming in on Anika's blog."

"You're subscribed to it?" exclaimed Jazz.

"It's really exciting!" Mack protested.

"Well, don't let me stop you from reading some more," said Jazz sarcastically.

"I don't want to look yet," Mack admitted as they

reached Anika's house. "I haven't read her last post because I was busy with our science project last night."

Jazz rolled her eyes and was about to chide Mack again for her obsession with schoolwork when she stopped in her tracks on the Belmonts' veranda.

"Wait," Jazz said, pausing at the sight of the front door of Anika's place, usually firmly locked, standing wide open. She slipped the unneeded key back into her pocket and looked down the side of the house. "Look, both Anika's parents' cars are still in the driveway."

"Do you think something's wrong?" asked Mack, her eyes showing concern. Wordlessly, the two girls went inside. Hearing sounds of distress, they rushed to the living room. Mr. Belmont stood gazing at his phone, gaping in shock. Mrs. Belmont, both hands covering her face, sobbed so violently that her whole body shook.

"Mrs. Belmont! What's happened? Mr. Belmont? What is it? Where's Anika?" Jazz asked through a lump in her throat. Both girls' eyes, frightened and bewildered, were riveted on the adults.

"Oh, Jazz!" Mrs. Belmont cried, grabbing her in a hug. "It's Anika! She's—" Mrs. Belmont broke off into more uncontrollable sobs.

"She's been kidnapped!" Mr. Belmont said numbly.

Jazz and Mack stared at each other in horror.

"You have to tell the police!" said Jazz.

"We can't," said Mrs. Belmont. "The kidnapper just called. They said no police . . ."

"But . . ." Mack protested.

Mr. Belmont shook his head. "They said it *three times.* We can't risk our daughter's life like that! If we want to get her back safely, we have to wait for them to text us, then do exactly what they say!"

Jazz's ears pricked up. "'They'? Was the voice a man's or woman's?"

"We couldn't tell," said Mrs. Belmont. "It was a strange raspy voice. Oh, this is a nightmare!" she moaned.

The Belmonts, faces white, sank to the sofa and huddled there, overcome.

Jazz stood frozen, stunned. Anika—her oldest friend— kidnapped! A horrible feeling of regret washed over her. The last conversation they'd had was that stupid fight about the blog! Jazz wished more than anything that she could take everything she had said back.

The sound of a phone alert snapped everyone to attention.

They all huddled around Mr. Belmont to see the text message he had just received. For a moment he simply stared at the phone, as if frightened by what it might contain.

"Hurry up!" Mrs. Belmont cried.

Opening the message, Mr. Belmont's brows knotted in confusion. "It's a web address," he said.

Jazz leaned in closer and swiftly memorized the address.

"Where does it lead? What does it say?" Mrs. Belmont asked frantically as she and her husband exchanged fearful glances. He pressed on the link. Anika's parents, and Jazz and Mack all held their breath looking at the phone screen as the site loaded.

It was a blog, with a single entry:

> **> IDENTITY WITHHELD <**
>
> Somewhere hidden in your house, there is a small wooden jewelry box with the initials LT on it. When you find it, leave a comment below describing what you can see in the box, but DO NOT TOUCH anything inside it. A new post will then give you further instructions.
>
> Your daughter will be safe if you do as you are told.
>
> YOU HAVE UNTIL MIDNIGHT TOMORROW.
>
> ## IF YOU CALL THE POLICE I WILL KNOW!

The last line of the message made Jazz shudder. *Could they be watching us or monitoring the house, right now?* she wondered.

Jazz walked over to the large glass doors that overlooked the back terrace and garden. Methodically, she noted what surrounded the Belmonts' house on each side. On the eastern border, above tall palm trees, she could see two of the windows of the upper story of Deepwater, the spooky mansion next door. On the other side, the neighbor's house was hidden behind the tall fence that ran around the Belmonts' backyard, apart from a gable window that poked out from the roof. She took out her phone to take pictures.

"Jazmine, what are you doing?" Mr. Belmont called sternly. He ran over and grabbed her phone from her hands. "You can't post online about this! This is a matter of life or death!"

"I wouldn't!" said Jazz, dismayed.

"Promise me," he said. "Jazmine, Mackenzie, you mustn't tweet or post about this. We told you what the kidnapper said. We have to handle this ourselves. Anika's life depends on it."

39:35

"**W**e have to find that box," Mrs. Belmont said. She searched the room, lifting cushions, peering into lamps and other items, no matter how unlikely.

Jazz started to look for it as well but noticed Mack heading for the front door and beckoning her to follow.

"Mack, where are you going? We've got to help Anika's mum and dad find the jewelry box," Jazz said as they walked outside.

"I think we need to let her parents have some time alone," said Mack. "This must be so hard. We can come back after school if they still haven't found the box."

"School?" cried Jazz. "I can't go to school. No way could I concentrate on anything. All I can think of is Anika."

"I can't miss class."

"How can you think about school at a time like this?"

THE VANISHING

Mack looked away, her face lined with distress. "I'd like to help you, Jazz. I care about Anika; she's my best friend too. But my parents would kill me. They've got enough to stress about without me ditching school to track down a kidnapper."

"But, Mack! This is really important! Anika, your *friend*, is missing and is probably in terrible danger!"

Tears streamed down Mack's face. "I know that, but I have to go. What could we do here, anyway? We might even get in the way. You may have read a lot of true-crime stories, Jazz, but that doesn't give you real-life experience."

A car drove past and slowed as it approached the Belmonts' house. Jazz watched it closely, noting its color, the make and model, and its license plate. She tensed as it pulled up outside Anika's house. Was this something to do with the kidnapping? She started to get out her phone to take a picture of the suspect when . . .

A security guard got out and went into Deepwater.

Jazz sighed and turned back to Mack. "What I do know is that the first **48 HOURS** matter."

"Why?"

"The first **48 HOURS** are the best time to gather evidence—before the trail runs cold and important clues get moved or whatever. What I'm saying, Mack, is that you're right: the Belmonts can look for the box. But we both heard them say they're not even going to call the police. Nobody else is going to investigate this. *We* need to find out who the kidnapper is. I mean, even if the Belmonts do find the box, how do we know if the kidnapper'll ever bring her back?" Jazz shivered.

"We don't," whispered Mackenzie.

"Mack, that's why we *have* to find out what happened to Anika. Who took her and why, and bring her home safely. And do it within **48 HOURS**. I need your brain power! Will you help me?"

Mack blew her nose and allowed herself a small smile. "I can help you."

Jazz relaxed. "So you'll be my partner?"

Mack shook her head. "Not me, but I can think of a great partner for you. And a much smarter option than me. You need the most brilliant brain in the hood to help you. Someone who can not only hack a website but also get you into a professional lab." Mackenzie couldn't help but grin as she said, "If you're going to investigate this crime, you're going to need Phoenix Lyons."

"Phoenix?" Jazz cried, incredulous. "You're joking. No way, Mack! I'm never going to ask for his help. Not in a million years!"

39:19

Phoenix Lyons was fighting to save himself. Flicking his hair out of his eyes, he put his clenched hands in front of his face, and braced himself for the next assault.

"Think you're tough, do ya?" mocked his opponent. "Then let's see what you've got."

His attacker came at him faster than he'd expected and Phoenix found himself backed into a corner, dodging blows.

"Come on, would ya, fight back! Whaddaya scared or something?"

Phoenix tried to block out the taunts and concentrate on his counterattack. He struck out with a quick one-two jab, putting all the desperate weight of his body behind the punch. The momentum carried him and he tumbled forward. *I won't fall*, he told himself as he tried to correct his dangerous angle, hearing his attacker close in on him. *I won't.*

Instead, he managed to steady himself and change the fall into a turn, spinning around to take his opponent by surprise and deliver a solid body blow that dropped him to the floor. Phoenix stood there, panting.

His opponent stared up at him, then a big grin split his tanned face, crinkling up his blue eyes. He put up a gloved hand, which Phoenix took.

"Phoenix! Well done, mate!"

Phoenix returned the grin as he helped his boxing coach, Simon, to his feet.

"That was a great combo. You kept your balance and turned defense into attack."

Phoenix and Simon stepped out of the ring, sipping water as they caught their breath. Phoenix had met Simon here at the gym about a year ago, when he'd started up casual boxing lessons. Since he'd been suspended, he'd ramped up the sessions till he was heading to the gym on a daily basis.

"Your style is really improving," Simon said. "It reminds me of something my dad used to say: *If you can't walk away from a fight, take it on with everything you've got!*"

"My dad has a saying too," scowled Phoenix. "*If you*

can walk away from a fight, do."

Since coming to the gym, Phoenix had talked a lot about his dad, telling Simon stuff he'd never share with his friends. Like how distant his dad was. Mr. Lyons was always working and never home. He only seemed to care about what Phoenix was doing when he got in trouble. And his mum was just as bad, focused on her work. At least she was home more, but that was only because her forensics business was based there. His parents had put an extension on the house and equipped it with a professional lab. But that now meant his mum worked even longer hours there than his dad did at the bank.

"I gotta say, mate," Simon was speaking now, "it sounds like you've been taking your dad's advice."

Phoenix stopped mid sip, his granite eyes glaring at Simon. "What does that mean?"

"You're still suspended, and you hang around here every day. Maybe you're avoiding something. Aren't you just supposed to write a letter so they'll let you go back to school?"

Phoenix toweled the sweat off his short dark hair and slicked it back. "Maybe I don't wanna go back."

Simon smirked. "Having too much fun, eh?"

Phoenix took a long drink, stung by Simon's words. He knew the instructor was teasing him, but Simon was so close to the truth he couldn't think of a comeback.

"I'll catch ya tomorrow," Simon said. "Unless you're back at school." He gave Phoenix a fist bump and started getting ready for his next student.

* * *

Phoenix headed for the harbor after he left the gym. Kicking an empty oyster shell along the boardwalk, he saw a couple of old blokes with caps on their heads, sleeves rolled up, and a bait bucket between them. They sat on the jetty's edge, fishing and talking companionably. Out on the water, ferries cut through the low chop, carrying people from the suburbs to the central business district. Phoenix was in no hurry to get home. Did that mean that what Simon had said was true? Was he avoiding a confrontation with his parents?

Hacking into the school's computer system had been the most exciting thing he'd done in a while. Part of him had thought his parents would recognize the skill that it took. He'd even thought they might be proud! Instead, when they found out, they just went on about him having to grow up and learn some responsibility. He'd been given a list of jobs to do around the house and garden, mowing the lawn, weeding, hosing out the trash cans—which he'd ignored. Then they'd left him to his own devices, not even asking what he'd been doing all day.

He hated to say it, but Phoenix sometimes wondered if his hacking prank had even been worth it. He spent most of his days at the gym, or in his bedroom, programming. His friends were all at school and there was often no reply to his texts and memes. Being suspended was boring.

He'd never admit it to anyone—even Simon—but he actually *missed* school. Missed being the smartest in the class, missed hanging out with his mates. He could go back tomorrow if he just wrote the letter, but it was getting harder and harder to do. He almost wished he'd done it straightaway. Now it was a matter of pride.

As he walked along the street he thought to himself, *I did them a favor proving how insecure their computer system is. They should thank me!*

He started up the walkway to his house, then turned, hearing someone yelling out his name.

"Phoenix? Phoenix Lyons!"

A girl was running toward him, waving, her blonde hair flying. Suddenly his day was looking up. Phoenix patted his hair to make sure it was sitting how he liked it, then slouched near the mailbox, trying to look casual.

He squinted at the approaching figure, and his cool expression vanished. *Oh no! Not her!* He groaned inwardly. *Not Jazz Mandell.* She danced around the room every time she beat him on a math test (which wasn't that often, he reminded himself). She was some kind of budding amateur detective and always interrupted science class to ask the teacher something about forensic analysis. Since she'd found out his mum was *actually* a forensic scientist, he'd actively tried to avoid her. Why would she be ditching school to find *him*?

As she caught up to him, puffing, he saw with surprise that she'd been crying. She was trying to hide it, looking down at the ground rather than straight at him, but it was obvious.

"Phoenix, I need your help!"

Phoenix wondered if he should ask what was wrong. Then he remembered his mantra: cool and nonchalant.

"I don't do tutoring. There are lots of good math websites if you want help," he said casually.

Jazz glared at him, her blue eyes suddenly clear and angry. "I'm not asking for tutoring," she said. "I'd rather not ask you for anything, ever, but this is really serious. Anika's life might depend on it!"

"What are you talking about?" Phoenix raised an eyebrow.

"First you have to swear to total secrecy."

Phoenix rolled his eyes. "If you want me to join some kind of secret club, sorry, I don't have time for that kind of thing. Maybe you should ask one of your girlfriends. Unless they're not talking to you or something?" He turned and walked toward the house, trying to ignore the niggling truth that if there was anything he had in abundance right now, it was time.

Jazz came after him, pulling on his sleeve. "That's just it! You don't have to like me and I don't have to like you, but I need your help! We have to collect evidence, find the clues and investigate what has happened. Oh, and I'll need access to your mum's lab so I can do the samples analysis. I mean *we'll* need it—please, you have to help me, Phoenix!"

"You're not making any sense," Phoenix shouted at her, confused and annoyed. "Why would I let you into my mum's lab? Is that what this is about? Why don't you stop playing games and go back to school?" He turned back toward his house and started walking away.

"Phoenix Lyons! Listen to me!" Jazz screeched at his back. She strode toward him and took a breath. More calmly and quietly she said, "What's the use of having a brilliant mind like yours if you don't use it to do something really good? Please, just look at this!" Jazz held out her phone, a website displayed on the screen. The URL caught his eye.

"That's a heavily encrypted site," Phoenix said, intrigued despite himself. He read the post then looked at Jazz. The cool, nonchalant expression had vanished. Now Phoenix looked stunned. "What is this?"

Jazz took a breath, clearly relieved to finally have his attention. "You know Anika Belmont? She lives around the corner from here."

Phoenix nodded.

"She was taken—kidnapped—last night, from her own room! The kidnapper sent her parents that message this morning. They're too scared to call the police. I need your help to investigate who took Anika and help me find her. Please, Phoenix."

He looked again at Jazz, seeing the fear and distress in her eyes. Phoenix could see now that Jazz wasn't messing around. This was no game. This was for real, and very bad. He noticed his heart racing and his senses quickening. He felt more alive than he had in days.

"She's my best friend," Jazz continued. "Believe me, I wouldn't normally say this, but I need your help. I need you to help me find her."

Phoenix took a deep breath. He couldn't deny it; it was the best offer he'd had all day. All week. Actually, all his life. Phoenix leveled his gray eyes at her and after a pause said, "OK, where do we start?"

Jazz grinned and said, "I almost feel like hugging you. Almost."

38:26

"**F**irst things first," Phoenix said, "we need to get supplies."

"Supplies? You're just like my brother, always thinking about food. We don't have time."

"Not those kind of supplies," said Phoenix. "Swabs, evidence bags, we need to grab what we can from my mum's lab. And we need to act fast so we can get the physical evidence from the PLS. That's the—"

"Point Last Seen, I know," smiled Jazz. "Math isn't the only thing I can beat you in, Phoenix."

"Watch it," said Phoenix. "Do you want these supplies or not?"

Jazz put her hands up in mock surrender, and quickly followed as Phoenix hurried around to the back gate. As he let himself in via the glass doors at the back of the house, Jazz looked around. There was a patio and swimming pool surrounded by palm trees.

"Where are your parents?" she asked as she headed inside.

"Mum's car's not here, although usually she works at home in the lab," Phoenix explained. "Dad's at work. As usual. And he won't be back until really late. Still, we have to be quick. Mum could be back at any moment."

Jazz noticed Phoenix seemed nervous as he grabbed a large empty sports bag and beckoned her to follow him through the house. He kept craning his neck to look out the windows to the front driveway.

"So your mum really lets you borrow stuff from her lab?" she asked.

"Um, yeah, sure, I do it all the time. This way," he said. Jazz followed him through the house until they came to a large fireproof door with an electronic lock. "The lab's through there," he said. Jazz watched carefully as he entered a six-digit code on the electronic keypad. "We need to get some PPE."

"PPE?"

"You don't know?" Phoenix smirked, as the door swung open to his touch. "It means Personal Protective Equipment. Guess it helps to have some contact with *real* forensics."

Jazz made a face behind his back, already wondering if getting him to help was such a great idea.

They stepped into a long room housing tall lockers and several white coats hanging from hooks. Four pairs of rubber boots stood neatly beneath them.

"This is the clean room. The actual lab is through that door," he said. Jazz noticed how a fan had started up the moment he unlocked the door. The clean room smelled of antiseptic and bleach. "If we're going to investigate a crime scene like Anika's room," said Phoenix, "we've got to be properly outfitted. We can't contaminate it."

"I know that," Jazz said, annoyed. "But we have to be quick." She glanced at her phone. **9:36 AM**. "The clock is ticking on the first **48 HOURS**."

"What's this first **48 HOURS** you so subtly brought up?" asked Phoenix, unzipping the empty sports bag and opening one of the tall lockers.

"You don't know?" mimicked Jazz. "Guess it helps to read books too."

"Oh, yeah? And what do your books tell you?"

"That the first **48 HOURS** after a crime has been committed are vital to collecting the freshest and most useful evidence."

Phoenix handed her what looked like folded sheets but turned out to be a pair of white coveralls complete with a hood. It was the sort of gear worn by forensic service personnel. Hair coverings, thin rubber gloves and booties followed. There were sterile swabs in sealed, single-use packs, together with a box of ready-to-use sealable plastic tubes. She put it all in the sports bag.

"Equipment. That's what's vital to collecting the 'freshest and most useful evidence,'" Phoenix teased.

"What exactly does your mum do again?" Jazz asked, peering around Phoenix to get a closer look inside the lab itself.

"Mum runs a private chemical analysis lab," he explained. "She consults for the police on investigations and does work for environmental agencies too."

"So she does fingerprint checking and DNA analysis?" asked Jazz.

"Yeah, lots of that, and checking out microscopic samples from arson sites and crime scenes. Sometimes she does handwriting analysis, or examines a document or check to see if it's been forged."

"You'll never be able to get away with forging her signature on a note then!" Jazz grinned.

"I could actually," said Phoenix, not getting the joke. "I'm especially talented with tracing paper and a backlight."

Phoenix took two containers of what looked like black dust and white dust and a small, soft brush from a cabinet next to the lockers and added them to the stash in the large bag.

"Let's go," he said.

Phoenix led Jazz back through the house and outside. They set out for Anika's at a fast pace.

Jazz felt a mixture of fear and excitement about the prospect of helping to find Anika. "So what's the plan when we get there?" she asked.

"Examine the scene? Take samples? Sorry, you were there a minute ago when we grabbed all the equipment, right?"

"I'm not talking about the forensics; I'm talking about Anika's parents."

"What about them?"

"Oh, so we just barge in on two distraught parents and say, 'Hi, mind if we swab for DNA?'"

"Good point, actually; we'll need to get elimination samples from the whole family."

"You're unbelievable," she said as they reached Anika's house.

"Aren't you going to knock?" asked Phoenix, after they had been standing on the porch for a few seconds.

"It just feels so weird. I always let myself straight in."

"You mean they don't lock their door?" said Phoenix. "Well, that's the first stage of forensic examination finished—point of entry. The kidnapper could have just walked straight in."

"Well, my first rule of investigation is 'know the victim.' Mr. and Mrs. Belmont are really strict about security and *always* lock this front door. I come here every day so I have my own key."

"Whatever," said Phoenix, impatiently. "Just knock already."

Anika's mum opened the door. The look of disappointment that replaced the hope in her eyes was heartbreaking. Mrs. Belmont forced her tearstained face into a smile. "Jazz, dear, I know you must be worried, but I'm not sure this is a good time to be visiting. Unless, do you know anything about this—this jewelry box that the kidnapper wants? Did Anika say anything about it to you?"

Sensing her opportunity, Jazz pushed the front door open farther and stepped inside, aware of Phoenix following close behind her. Mrs. Belmont didn't even seem to notice him as she went to the hall closet and started searching among the jackets and umbrellas inside.

"No," said Jazz, shaking her head. "Never." She glanced at Phoenix, who seemed engrossed in something on the ceiling. She was about to ask Mrs. Belmont if she could get her a drink or some food when Phoenix spoke abruptly.

"Where's your CCTV monitor?"

Mrs. Belmont looked at him, confused. He pointed up at a discreet camera over the front door.

"We'll need to review the footage," he said. Noticing Jazz's furious face, he added, "If that's OK and everything."

Mrs. Belmont nodded and waved them vaguely down the hall toward a dark-green room. Long curtains brushed the floorboards. A leather chair stood in front of a large desk that supported a powerful computer along with a huge high-tech monitor showing footage from the Belmont's top-end security system.

Jazz was too antsy to sit down, but Phoenix was in his element among all that technology. He whistled appreciatively, grabbed the monitor remote and sprawled back in the luxurious swivel chair. He selected the CCTV record from last night and started playing the various camera angles on fast-forward. The split screen showed views from cameras mounted over the front and back doors of the house, a view up the staircase, and a long view taking in the upstairs hall from which the bedrooms opened.

As Phoenix whizzed through footage of the early

evening, Jazz's heart skipped a beat. She saw Anika practicing a long jump in the upstairs hallway, checking her distance on the floorboards, ponytail swinging as she landed.

As Phoenix continued zooming through the various camera angles from throughout the night, Jazz watched intensely, waiting for a sign of whoever had taken her best friend.

But her expectation turned to disappointment. When all the tape had been reviewed, Phoenix turned to her, eyebrows raised. "OK. What do you make of that?" he asked.

"Nobody came into the house," said Jazz, incredulously. "Not by the front door, not by the back door, and certainly nobody came up the staircase or along the hall."

"And no one went out either, including Anika. So, the big question is, how was Anika taken?"

"Do you think it might mean something—some *thing*—took her?"

"Something not human? Undetectable by CCTV? Is that what you're suggesting?"

"I know it sounds crazy."

"It *is* crazy. Sherlock Holmes used to say that once you've eliminated the impossible—alien abduction, teleportation and so on—what remains, no matter how improbable, must be the truth."

"Oh, so you *do* read?! OK, Sherlock. So?"

"Well, *Watson*, there's got to be another way in—and out."

"How? Where?"

"When we track down the kidnapper, we'll ask them," said Phoenix, winding the tapes back.

"Let's focus on the external footage," said Jazz, unsure if Phoenix was mocking her or not. "Because even if there's a way in that we don't know about, the kidnapper would still have to approach the house some way."

"This must be the most boring job in the world," Phoenix muttered. Jazz was about to retort when something on the screen caught her eye.

"Look!" she exclaimed. "You can just see something there near the middle of the frame. A blurry movement. What is it?"

"The CCTV cameras did pick up someone after all."

"Give me that," Jazz said, grabbing the remote. She froze the sequence, frame by frame, until she came to the best view. They peered at it together.

"It looks like an oddly bulky leg—in a boot," said Phoenix, head to one side. "But what sort of leg is *that*?"

"See! It doesn't look human," Jazz said triumphantly.

Phoenix rolled his eyes.

Jazz checked the timer in the corner of the footage: **12:01 AM**. She checked her watch—they'd lost over ten of the first **48 HOURS** already!

"Enough TV watching," Phoenix said, as he jumped up from the chair. "We need to get up to the Point Last Seen."

37:40

"This way," said Jazz, leading Phoenix up the stairs. They walked down the hallway they'd just seen on camera. One that Jazz had walked down so many times before. But this felt different. Jazz stopped as they reached Anika's room. It looked so familiar. The walls were covered with posters of Anika's favorite bands and ribbons from sports triumphs. Jazz looked at the rug she'd sat on countless times, laughing and talking. She glanced at the corkboard over the desk and saw dozens of photos of her and Anika smiling back at her. Mack too. Long drapes hung over the tall window where she and her best friend had loved to gaze over at Deepwater. They liked to imagine the manor's great hall in its prime, hosting elegant balls with dancers in fancy dresses.

THE VANISHING

Jazz became aware of Phoenix holding the PPE out to her. She took the white suit and booties and started putting them on over her clothes and shoes. For all its familiarity, today this wasn't the bedroom of a friend. Today, she was a crime-scene examiner.

"Where do we start?" Jazz mumbled, as much to herself as to Phoenix. She pulled her tablet from her bag and opened up CrimeSeen. She couldn't believe that the real investigation she was finally getting to track was the kidnapping of her own best friend.

A hint popped up on screen:

Jazz started photographing the room from every angle. She panned around, recording video, stopping as Phoenix came into the shot, looking at her with a bemused smile.

"If I wanted to play computer games, I could have stayed at home," he said.

"You think this is a game?" cried Jazz. "My best friend is missing! Forgive me if I don't intend to rely just on what you've 'picked up' from your mum."

"OK, super sleuth," he said. "Look around. What do you see that's out of the ordinary? Anything that shouldn't be here. Or anything that should be here—but isn't."

Stepping carefully over to Anika's desk, Jazz couldn't help but think of the morning before, when she and Mack had come to pick up Anika. Jazz had given her friend such a hard time, when all Anika wanted to do was finish a few more lines of her blog about the stupid journal. Tears pricked her eyes again.

Wait, the journal! she thought.

"The journal's not here!" she cried.

"What journal?" Phoenix asked.

"Anika found this old journal—some woman's diary— hidden behind that mirror. She became completely crazy about it. She blogged about it every day, putting extracts from it online. It was always here, just on her desk, next to her laptop."

"What was in it?" Phoenix probed.

Jazz felt fresh tears. "I never read it," she said quietly. "We actually fought about it. It seems so stupid now! She said I didn't appreciate the magic of it—that all I wanted to do was pull it apart for clues. I thought she was being silly so I refused to read any of it. All I know is that it was old and apparently written by a woman and there was some big mystery—even a crime maybe."

Phoenix frowned. "Why would the kidnapper take the journal?"

"There must have been something in it—something that made him want it."

"We are presuming it's a 'he'?"

Jazz shrugged. "According to my books, they often are."

"So why didn't 'he' take the jewelry box at the same time as the journal?"

"Something went wrong," Jazz said, thinking aloud. "Maybe they were interrupted. Or they couldn't find it."

Phoenix nodded. "When Mrs. Belmont asked you before if you knew anything about the jewelry box, you said no. Is that true?"

"Of course it is! Why would I lie to her, especially when this has happened?!"

"OK, OK. I just assumed that you and Anika would

have told each other everything."

"Anika never mentioned a box. Then again, I didn't exactly make it easy for her to tell me anything about it."

"All right, let's get on to collecting the samples to analyze back at the lab. Watch what I do and then do the same to all the surfaces, like areas around the bed, the desk and from the rug and the floorboards."

Jazz nodded, eager to get started.

Phoenix opened the sports bag to reveal the sterile tubes he'd collected. "These are already robot ready," he said.

"Robots?" said Jazz. "You have robots in the lab?"

"Not the sort you're thinking about. But automated programs," Phoenix explained. "Once we've taken our swabs, they go into these containers which are self-sealing. Then we record the date and place, describe whereabouts in the room they came from and initial them." He handed Jazz a pen. "There are two types of swabs: one type has already been prepared for collecting DNA, while the other type is plain. The second one acts as a control and we need both of them. Then all I have to do is put them in Mum's new DNA analysis program, and the results print out at the other end." He couldn't resist adding, "Right up to the offender's name and address."

"Wow! That is brilliant," said Jazz, before she realized

from the smarmy expression on his face that he was teasing her about the last part. "Idiot!" she whispered.

Phoenix went around the room and swabbed the knobs on Anika's chest of drawers, using a DNA-ready swab as well as the plain, control one. Then he moved onto the headboard, the bedside table, the door handle, and the desk, labeling each sample with the location from which it had been taken. Jazz was doing the same, taking swabs with gloved hands, then carefully sealing them in and labeling the tubes.

Jazz did a mental calculation of all the surfaces in the room. No wonder the experts insisted on the importance of gathering evidence as soon as possible. This was going to take a long time.

"We also need to take fiber lifts," said Phoenix, "using this adhesive tape." He demonstrated, pressing the tape firmly along the surface of the desktop, then gently peeling it off with tweezers and placing the fibers from it into the smaller sterile tubes, before sealing them. Jazz did the same. On the label, following Phoenix's example, she wrote:

> RUG, LEFT-HAND SIDE
> OF BED

Soon she had quite a collection of tape lifts sealed and annotated.

On one tape, among several long dark hairs, Jazz noticed a much shorter, paler hair. *Whose hair is that?* she wondered. Anika's hair was a vibrant dark brown, as was her dad's. Her mum's was a shoulder-length stylish gray. It was too short to be one of her own long blonde hairs, and it was definitely not one of Mack's. Carefully, she lifted it off the tape and put it into a tube.

As she took the last of the fiber lifts from the rug, she found another mysterious hair, that was different again, and added it to her collection.

"Now we dust for fingerprints," Phoenix said. He started twirling a fine-haired brush over the black dust he'd carefully sprinkled on the surfaces of Anika's desk and bedside table.

Jazz caught a side view of Phoenix's face, frowning in concentration, edged by the white hood covering his head. She had to admire his methodical approach.

"Look!" Jazz said excitedly. "I can see prints here. And here. And over there. That fingerprint dust is making them visible."

"My guess is that those belong to Anika, because they're everywhere. What we are looking for is one that's different. But we won't know until we get back to the lab where I can load them into a program and zoom in on them."

Phoenix worked steadily, photographing the prints revealed by the black dust. "I've just realized that for the first time since my suspension, I'm happy. We're doing something important, something that might help crack a very serious crime. Something that my dad might be proud of. This is much better than hacking into the school's computer system." Phoenix abruptly stopped speaking.

Jazz straightened up from her work, and saw Phoenix was blushing, as if he was embarrassed to have said so much.

"I agree with you," she said. "I'm really glad you're helping me do something to help Anika." And she was. The feeling of total helplessness had gone, replaced with a small but growing hope that between her knowledge and Phoenix's access to equipment, they would be able to help bring Anika home.

They continued their work companionably. As she added the date to another sample, Jazz became aware of Phoenix standing quite still near her. "What is it?" she asked, looking up to find him staring at Anika's photo board.

"Just seeing all these photos of Anika doing stuff, it

became a bit more . . . *real* . . . to me." Phoenix shrugged. "I got a bit caught up in the process, and forgot that there are people involved."

Jazz nodded. "She's a really great friend. She's fun and noisy, and a great sprinter—" Jazz looked at the ribbons and trophies displayed around the room "—even though she's only tiny. Not like me." Jazz glanced at her tall body in the mirror and noticed that there were tears in her eyes. As she reached for a tissue, a floorboard creaked under her feet. "Anika reckons that floorboard only squeaks when *I* step on it, but I think she just avoids it so her folks don't know when she's sneaking downstairs for snacks."

She went to throw the tissue in the trash.

"Wait, I might need that for a sample," said Phoenix.

Jazz froze. "You are joking, right?"

A grin broke Phoenix's usually sullen face. "Of course I am. A cheek scraping will be fine."

Jazz noticed something as she dropped the tissue in the trash. She bent down closer. "Look," she said, pointing to the paneling near the floor. "Something's wrong here."

"You're right." Phoenix leaned over. "This panel looks like it's lifting away from the wall."

Phoenix started yanking the panel hard toward him.

He almost fell backward as it pulled away easily.

Jazz stared in astonishment. Instead of wall behind the panel, there was nothing—just a dark, gaping hole in the masonry.

"No way! The kidnapper must have tunneled in!" Jazz exclaimed.

Phoenix shook his head. "To the second floor? This is no tunnel. This was already here." He examined the panel, which was fitted with a sturdy handle on the inside.

Jazz gasped. "A laundry chute!" Her mind went back to *Crimes that Stopped the Nation*. "I read about a robbery where the burglars came in via a laundry chute. They had them in old houses to push all the washing down into these huge ceramic tubs. The burglars tried to get off by claiming it wasn't technically a break-in!"

"Thanks for the history lesson," joked Phoenix. "I'm going to get a better look." He climbed up onto the bottom edge of the masonry and peered into the dark hole. "I think I can see some faint light right at the bottom," he said. But as he leaned farther, aiming the light on his phone with his extended arm, stretching out as far as possible in order to see where the laundry chute ended, his feet slipped from the narrow ledge. Phoenix overbalanced, clawed wildly at the empty air, and fell into the darkness.

37:00

Jazz heard a bang and a thud.

She froze. *I hope he's OK*, she thought. *He made a lot of noise. Surely the Belmonts must have heard that?* She tiptoed to the door, but all was quiet and still.

Going back over to the hole in the wall, she called down as loudly as she dared, not wanting to unduly worry Anika's already distraught parents. "Phoenix! Are you OK?"

"Bit dusty," he called back up. "Are you going to join me?"

"I think I'll take the easy way down—you know, stairs and doors."

"At least we know how the kidnapper got in and out!"

"Are you crazy? They would have woken up the house falling down there."

"Look again, Watson," said Phoenix, shining the light from his phone on the walls of the chute. Uneven brickwork had left handy foot grips at regular intervals.

"You wanted an easy way out," teased Phoenix. "Come on down!"

Jazz clenched her fists in annoyance. But she didn't want Phoenix to see she was afraid of the small, dark space and of slipping off the brickwork. So she gritted her teeth, put the bag over one shoulder and climbed into the chute, clinging awkwardly to the walls. She tried not to think about Phoenix staring at her backside the whole time she climbed down.

"What took you so long?" Phoenix grinned at her from where he stood in the old laundry. She smirked back at him when she saw his face, streaked with dirt and with a large smudge on his nose that made him look a bit like a pug.

"Very funny, Phoenix," she said, reaching for an old towel hanging on a hook. "You look like a—"

Phoenix hissed, "Stop right there. Don't take another step. We might destroy evidence."

Despite the dim light coming through the grimy windows, clear footprints were visible on the dusty laundry floor. The marks were either left by someone with a big shoe size or someone wearing boots. They appeared to go in both directions.

"That's got to be our kidnapper!" Jazz said.

"I'd say it's a good bet," Phoenix replied. He pulled a small can out of the bag and gave it a shake.

Jazz couldn't suppress a laugh. "You carry *hair spray* with you?"

"Not for hair," he said, flicking his back. "It's a good fixative."

He crouched to spray the prints, then moved around carefully, taking photos of the marks in the dust.

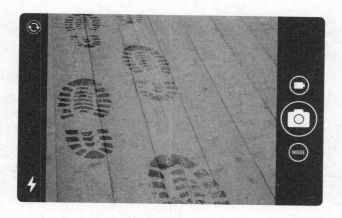

Then he stood up and leveled the camera at Jazz, quickly taking a shot before she could protest. He cackled as he checked his handiwork. "You look like a crazed panda!"

"Show me!" said Jazz, grabbing for the phone.

Phoenix turned the screen. Jazz was startled to see she'd somehow managed to get dirt into her eye sockets. A diagonal smear across her lower face gave the impression of a demented crooked grin.

"Put that online and I'll tell everyone you carry hair spray in your bag," she growled.

They looked around the dark and dusty room.

"I'm thinking this isn't where the Belmonts do their regular laundry, is it?" Phoenix asked.

"I didn't even know this room was here. They've got a laundry room upstairs."

Phoenix looked at her across dust motes dancing in the disturbed air. "You didn't know about it, but the kidnapper did. Not just the room, but the boarded-up chute as well."

"That means," said Jazz, thinking aloud, "that the kidnapper is someone who knows the house very well. It could be someone who lived here before the Belmonts bought the house. Or a tradesman."

Phoenix pushed his dark hair out of his eyes again and rubbed at the dirt on his cheek. "Or a member of the family."

Jazz shook her head vehemently. "No way. No one in Anika's family would do this. Besides, what would be the point? They could have taken the journal at any time."

"You're letting your emotions cloud your judgement," countered Phoenix. "The evidence points to an inside job."

"You're jumping to conclusions before considering all points of view," snapped Jazz. "Remember, it's not just Anika that the kidnapper was after—it's that jewelry box. What if taking Anika is just a diversion?"

"Well maybe there are some priceless jewels hidden in the box, and what if it's some poor relative of Anika's who's heard about them? They can't just start searching the house while they're visiting without raising suspicion, but if they took Anika and demanded the jewelry box in return for her safety, her parents would have to look for it. The kidnapper then gets the box, returns Anika, and—"

"—and that sounds way too complicated," said Jazz.

"Maybe. Investigators always have to keep an open mind. Haven't your books told you that?"

"OK, it's a possibility," admitted Jazz reluctantly as she followed Phoenix to the door.

Could their investigation really be leading them to someone Anika knew?

36:45

Creeping out through the old laundry door, the two investigators found themselves at the side of the house. They took off their protective gear and stuffed it into the Belmonts' trash can near the gate to the front driveway.

"No CCTV here," observed Jazz, looking up at the eaves. "But you wouldn't get through that gate without the camera at the front of the house picking it up."

"Then I say we go the other way," said Phoenix.

They scurried past the terrace along the back of the house. Phoenix trailed Jazz through a gate in the fence that separated the Belmont property from the derelict Deepwater mansion. A narrow overgrown strip of land ran between the Belmonts' fence and the old stone boundary walls of Deepwater. Weeds and grass grew between the stones, and in some places the wall had completely collapsed into a pile of broken sandstone rocks.

"Look," said Jazz, pointing to a couple of large deep footprints in some mud near the lowest part of the wall. "They look like the kidnapper's boot prints again. But where'd they go from here?"

"I have a hunch," said Phoenix, walking toward the derelict mansion's driveway. "Here!" he called. "You can see the impressions of a tire tread." They followed the treads over the uneven ground. In one area, where the tire had traveled over a sandy part of the driveway, it had left a very clear imprint. Phoenix photographed the lines of zigzag patterning carefully. "This is good," he muttered. "We might be able to match this to a database. I've got the Treadmate app. It matches tire prints to brands."

"You mean we might get an idea of what kind of vehicle the kidnapper used?"

"Yeah, well, I mean, the tires, at least."

The tire prints became fainter as they approached the heavily overgrown stone pillars and the rusting wrought iron gates where the driveway met the sidewalk next to the street. The gates were partly opened and quite immovable.

"Could a car even get through here?" wondered Jazz out loud.

"Only just," said Phoenix. "Look here." Phoenix directed her attention to some scratches in the rust on the right-hand gate. "Something's scraped past there."

Jazz looked closer. "You're right. I can see flecks of green paint caught in the rust." She turned to Phoenix. "Can we analyze them?"

"Yep, and I've got just the thing," he said. He pulled a little paintbrush and sterile tube from his sports bag and brushed some of the paint samples in.

"Hey! You kids!" An angry man, wearing dark jeans and a T-shirt with a security company's logo on the pocket, was storming down the driveway toward them.

"Security!" said Phoenix.

"This is private property!" yelled the man, thudding down closer to them. "What do you think you're doing?"

Under his stout belly, he wore a duty belt with a truncheon and a two-way radio. He had a mean expression on his face.

"There was a—a robbery next door," said Jazz, thinking fast, "and we're looking for clues."

"Were you here last night? Trespassing in that SUV?" the angry man questioned.

"What color was it?" Phoenix asked.

"I'm asking the questions here. So you're admitting it?" the security guy said.

"I'm not admitting anything at all. I don't have a green SUV," Phoenix answered.

"Just because you don't *own* one doesn't mean you didn't *steal* one."

"Oh, so it was green then?" Phoenix quipped.

The security guard was getting angrier. "How did you know that? Come on. I'm taking you down to the police station and you can tell the sergeant your tricky lies."

"No, you're not. We were just leaving!" said Jazz, breaking into a run. Together she and Phoenix thudded along the sidewalk toward the corner. "Where should we go?"

"Doesn't matter!" said Phoenix. "Let's put some distance between that security guy and us!"

Finally, three blocks away from the gates of Deepwater, they slowed down, puffing, and then stopped.

"I think we lost him," said Jazz, flinging herself down under a tree. She pulled out her tablet.

"You're stopping now?" asked Phoenix.

"I've got to note down everything we just found out. Better to do it straightaway before I forget anything."

She opened up CrimeSeen and started making notes.

CRIME SEEN | **NOTES**

11:45 AM

- CASE FILE
- NOTES
- EVIDENCE
- PROFILING
- CAMERA

KIDNAPPER

Mode of kidnapping: old laundry chute.

Kidnapper familiar with the house, even more familiar than the Belmonts.

Could it be:
a) previous occupant,
b) tradesman,
c) a family member?

Getaway vehicle: a green SUV.

"Ah, Jazz," said Phoenix. "You might want to hurry things up." He nodded his head down the block, where the security guard, red faced and wheezing, had just rounded the corner.

"Yikes!" Jazz cried, stuffing her tablet back into her bag. "Let's go!"

35:59

Running up the front walkway to his house, Phoenix was relieved to see his mum's car still wasn't back in the driveway. They'd be able to get straight into the lab and start looking at the samples they'd gathered. Fortunately, they'd lost the cranky security guard by leading him away from the area and then doubling back.

Jazz watched again as Phoenix punched in the code on the keypad to the clean room. Inside, Phoenix put on a hair cap and gloves. "Here," he said, thrusting a fresh set of PPE at Jazz and stepping into the lab with the bag of samples.

Once similarly outfitted, Jazz followed him into a long room that was filled with the kind of scientific equipment that she had never seen in the science laboratory at school. Jazz could recognize fume cupboards and Bunsen burners, and much of the glassware was familiar, but there were banks of gleaming white machines whose functions weren't immediately clear. It all looked very exciting.

"Wow, what's this?" breathed Jazz, pointing to what looked like a large white-hooded stove, except for a lidded housing area that had dozens of tiny wells in it. The whole system was connected to a TV monitor.

"That's the DNA sequencer," Phoenix said grandly. "Mum's latest acquisition."

He opened the bag, and Jazz saw straightaway that the small field-to-robot tubes containing the swabs from Anika's bedroom would fit perfectly into the machine's tiny wells.

"It's superfast and superaccurate. You don't have to prep the samples, which used to take hours," explained Phoenix. "They go directly into these wells and then the machine cycles through the DNA analysis automatically and prints out profiles for each individual you sampled so you can compare."

Jazz had read about this type of sequencer on one of the forensics blogs she followed. She was impressed that Dr. Lyons had one, and even more impressed that Phoenix could use it. She'd seen graphics of the printouts and knew they were very complicated.

"Great. Let's load it up then," said Jazz. She reached with her gloved hand into the sports bag's interior.

"Sure," said Phoenix. "I'll just, um, turn it on." He fiddled with some switches then said, "It'll take a while to boot up. We've got those hair samples, and some fingerprints. And that paint scraping we took. Why don't we work on those first?"

Phoenix switched on a stereoscopic light microscope as Jazz passed him the tube containing the green flakes of paint. Taking a clean glass slide from a pack on the lab bench, Phoenix sprinkled the paint scrapes onto the slide and then fixed it in position under the lenses of the microscope, peering down the eyepieces.

"Very interesting," he drawled. "You can see a little history in this paint."

"What do you mean?"

"See for yourself."

He moved away so that Jazz could position herself at the eyepieces of the microscope. The paint flakes, highly magnified now, revealed more about the car than they could have detected with the naked eye. Under the green was another layer of color, a dark red. She drew back, turning to Phoenix. "It's been repainted," she said. "A classic tactic for committing a crime using a stolen car!"

"Maybe," said Phoenix. "That dark red could also be rust proofing of some sort."

"So," said Jazz, "if we find a vehicle we think the kidnapper drove, and it has matching scrape marks on it, that would go a long way toward proving that the vehicle was there, next to the Belmonts' house."

Phoenix nodded. "It's a great clue."

"Can I get a screenshot of this?" asked Jazz.

"Sure," said Phoenix. He started fiddling with cables to plug the microscope into a monitor. "It's not going to make much of a screensaver, though."

"It's for my app."

"OK, let's look at those hair samples," said Phoenix, moving across to another complicated-looking piece of equipment. "This one's a comparison microscope," he explained. "We can view two samples, on two slides, at the same time for comparison."

Jazz passed him tubes containing lifts of Anika's hair along with the short, pale hair she had found. Phoenix took a small bottle from the shelf above the microscope.

"Clear nail polish?" Jazz asked in surprise. "Do you give manicures in here as well?"

"It's a good general mounting medium," he said, fixing the hairs in place with the clear lacquer, then deftly dropping a cover slide onto each. "There are specialized mounting fluids for different types of jobs, but nail polish is a good substitute."

He applied himself to the eyepieces and stared down. He drew back suddenly, frowning.

"What is it?" Jazz asked.

"Take a look at this," Phoenix said to Jazz. "The pale hair you found is on the right. Anika's is on the left. Tell me what you see."

Jazz moved into position behind the eyepieces of the microscope and peered down. It took her a moment to adjust to what she was seeing: two samples, on separate slides, in one field of vision, as if they were lying side by side. She cleared her throat. "I see two strands of hair, I think. Except one looks fairly smooth while the other one—the shorter one on the right— looks almost spiky, like there are lots of bits of hair stacked on one another."

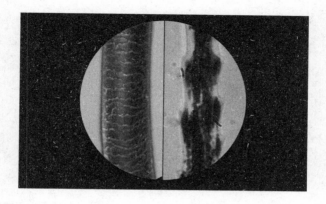

She straightened up and looked at Phoenix. "I didn't realize hairs could look so different from each other."

"One of them isn't a hair. At least, it's not a human hair."

For one crazy moment, Jazz got the image of some huge monster snatching up her friend in the middle of the night. She shook her head to get rid of the imagined horror. "So if it's not a human hair, what is it?"

"Could be from an animal. Does Anika have any pets?"

"Definitely not. She's been hassling her parents for a cat for ages, but—"

"Spare me the life story," said Phoenix. "Come over here. We'll do the fingerprints."

Phoenix plugged a cable from his phone into a computer flanked by two huge high-resolution monitors. He flicked through the photo album until he came to the fingerprints series, then selected all the shots and uploaded them. Once the analysis started, the program sorted through the dozens of thumbnail images, each one briefly displayed on the right-hand monitor in astonishing detail.

"It's finding matches," Phoenix explained. "The majority of prints we took were Anika's, and this can work out which prints are repeated over and over, then highlight any that are less frequent."

Jazz watched, fascinated and awed by the machine's processing power. Her reverie was shattered by a loud beep. The program had paused on a particular print, the words "**Error. Not recognized.**" flashing across the screen.

"What the . . . ?" said Phoenix, sitting up.

"No match?" suggested Jazz.

"It's no match for Anika's prints, or for any in the database," said Phoenix. "Check it out."

Jazz and Phoenix stared at the highly magnified image on the screen. The print had strange symmetrical crosshatching marks where whorls and ridges should have been.

Jazz broke the stunned silence: "What on earth made *that* print?"

"I can't believe I'm saying this again," said Phoenix, "but it's not a human fingerprint."

A sound nearby made them both jump back from the screen; someone was calling his name.

"Phoenix? Where are you?"

"Oh no!" Phoenix groaned. "Mum's looking for me."

"Great, maybe she can help work out where this fingerprint is from. Hey!" said Jazz, as Phoenix suddenly switched off the monitor and unplugged the data cable.

"Quick! Grab all this stuff! We've got to hide!"

Jazz watched, bemused, as Phoenix fumbled all the carefully sealed tubes into the sports bag along with his laptop, which he grabbed off the bench. "Over here!" he hissed, indicating the two closed doors of a cabinet on which the fume cupboard stood. He flung the bag into the cabinet and crawled in.

"Are you kidding?" said Jazz. "I'm not getting in there with you!"

Dr. Lyons was already at the clean-room door, punching in the key code.

"Maybe she's just coming in to pick something up quickly. Come *on!*" said Phoenix. Jazz saw his granite eyes pleading with her. She squeezed in beside him, squashed and bent like a rag doll. Phoenix pulled the doors closed but they didn't quite meet. He too was crushed into an uncomfortable ball.

They could just see a section of Dr. Lyons' white-coated figure through the tiny crack. She'd paused near the microscope. Jazz and Phoenix hoped his mother would stop looking and walk away. They breathed a silent sigh of relief as his mother moved away from the area in front of the microscope, but it was short-lived as she sat down at her desk.

"Now what?" Phoenix whispered.

All his mum would need to do to spot them was turn around. They were trapped. "We've got to get out of here," he hissed to Jazz. "Somehow."

Phoenix took a deep breath, and with great stealth, gently pressed one of the cabinet's doors open. Moving in slow motion, he put one leg out onto the floor followed by one hand and slowly, *slowly*, he slithered out, all the time staring at his mother, willing her to stay seated at her desk, with her back to them.

Jazz gently pushed the other door open and, staring fixedly at the back of Dr. Lyons' head, she too unfolded her cramped limbs and silently spilled onto the floor. Dr. Lyons moved in her chair and the two of them froze—then moved again as they saw she was simply reaching for a reference book on the shelf above her desk. They continued their stealthy slide across the floor, Phoenix taking agonizing care to make sure nothing clinked in the sports bag. Hearts pounding, they made it to the entrance to the clean room and Phoenix reached for the door handle.

Behind them, Dr. Lyons' chair scraped on the floor. *Don't get up now!* Phoenix begged. He slowly turned the handle then quietly pulled the door open, but there was a rushing sound of air as he did so. He grabbed Jazz and yanked her through the doorway, closing it behind him, wincing at the click it made. His mother must surely have heard that!

Phoenix didn't have to tell Jazz to hurry up. She was already pelting through the house, following him as they ran to the double doors and out into the backyard.

Once safely out of sight of the house, Jazz pulled off her hair cap and gloves and threw them at Phoenix. "What was all that about?" she yelled.

Phoenix bent to pick up the discarded items and

balled them together with his own.

"You told me your mum didn't mind you using the lab!" Jazz ranted.

"I knew her top secret code, didn't I?" Phoenix pouted.

"Pah!" said Jazz. "I watched you key it in—six digits? It was your birth date. Hardly top secret!"

"So? I still got us access to all the equipment!"

"Oh yeah, and just how does the DNA sequencer work? You don't know, do you?!"

"Do you?" Phoenix shot back. "What do you know about any of this? You've never even collected samples before. You need an app to tell you what to do!"

"I know that what you've done could put the whole case in jeopardy!"

"Oh, is it 'the case' now, big detective? I mean, really. What's your problem?" Phoenix asked.

"My problem? You lied to me! You pretended you could do something that you couldn't. We wasted time and time is everything right now. We've used up two hours of the first **48 HOURS** getting those samples and now we can't even do anything with them."

"Do it yourself, then. I've got better things to do than hang around here and be yelled at by you!"

Jazz wanted to storm off and forget she'd ever considered working with Phoenix. But then she thought of Anika—who needed her. And the evidence they still had to go through, and all that equipment in Dr. Lyons' lab. She had to work with him—for Anika's sake. She took a deep breath and ran her fingers through her hair, tucking it behind her ears.

"Phoenix, I probably can't do this without you as my partner, but I've got to be able to trust you. It's not going to work otherwise. This isn't some hacking job where you need to talk up your skills for your mates."

He stood there uncomfortably, head down until finally he spoke.

"I've heard Mum talking about running the DNA program lots of times. I really thought I could just copy what she did. But there's quite a bit of interpretation required in order to separate background DNA from the DNA that you're after and I forgot about that. And then I kind of got carried away. I wanted to do it properly, which we did; we did a good job at the crime scene . . ." He paused before adding, "I was keen to get back into the lab. I am allowed in there, honestly, but not since . . ."

"Since?" prompted Jazz.

"Since I got suspended. It's part of my punishment. No lab access until I write this stupid letter of apology to the principal."

"You think apologizing to the school for bringing down their entire network is stupid? Just write the letter already!" Jazz said, exasperated.

"I will, I will, OK?" said Phoenix. "But first of all, don't we have some investigating to do . . . partner?" He reached out a hand.

Jazz frowned. Perhaps Phoenix was being honest, but he was still a complete idiot at times. She couldn't deny it, though: she needed him. She just wished his ego didn't have to be part of the investigation as well.

Jazz took his hand and shook it. "We need somewhere to work," she said. "My brother's home and he'll be way too keen on a distraction from studying to leave us alone."

"That's OK. I think I know the perfect place."

34:45

Jazz heard the patter of leather on leather as Phoenix led her through a doorway marked SCHMICK N FIT.

"Are we here to work out?" she asked doubtfully.

"Nah, we've already gone a few rounds," Phoenix said with a chuckle. He waved at a stocky bloke pummeling a speed bag, whose sunburned face split into a grin under his ginger hair.

"The Phoenix rises again!" he quipped, coming over and grabbing Phoenix in a hug.

"Simon, this is Jazz," said Phoenix.

"Jazz, hi," said Simon, eyes twinkling as he shook her hand. "Are you here for boxing lessons too? You'll need to work hard to keep up with this guy—he can't stay away from the place!"

"Um, hi . . ." Jazz said, looking at Phoenix, surprised.

"We just need somewhere to work on an investi—" Phoenix felt a nudge from Jazz, "—on our homework."

"Homework, sure," said Simon, glancing from one to the other. "Partners in crime, eh?"

"Something like that," mumbled Phoenix. "Do you mind?"

"Course not! You can use the office. Dunno how much I can help, but if you need me, sing out."

Phoenix led the way to the back of the gym and into Simon's office. It was a neat room with a chair on each side of the desk. Training programs and diagrams of boxing moves were hung on the wall, along with a print of Muhammad Ali and his famous "butterfly" quote.

"Simon seems nice," said Jazz, as Phoenix grabbed them each a glass of water and settled himself at the desk. Getting no response, she added, "I didn't know you boxed."

"Most people don't," retorted Phoenix. "Guess I'm not one to talk myself up."

"Fine," said Jazz, not wanting to restart their argument. She sat down across from Phoenix. "Let's go over what we know. Can you shoot through the best images you've got?"

Jazz opened up CrimeSeen while Phoenix sent her the various photos he'd taken that morning along with the screenshots from the lab. Jazz started uploading the files as they came through and adding them to the app's evidence folder, drumming her fingers against the table as she waited.

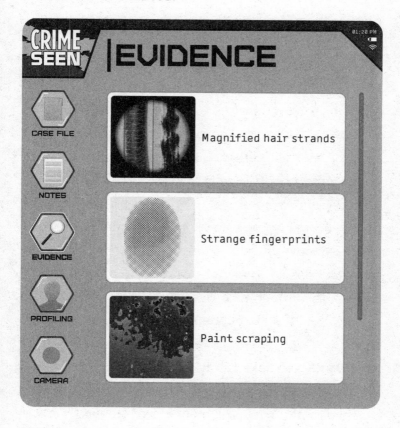

"OK," said Jazz. "Let's start with that alien fingerprint."

Phoenix brought up the image on his phone, side by side with one of Anika's prints. "It's all wrong," he mused.

"The lines of the ridges are crosshatched, not looped in a whorl like normal fingerprints. It's almost geometric. And it seems much bigger than a normal thumbprint."

"Remember that weird leg we saw on the CCTV footage?" offered Jazz. "It seemed enlarged too." Again she asked herself if some giant creature could be responsible for the kidnapping. Jazz recalled the cramped space of the laundry chute. *It can't have been too huge*, she thought.

Phoenix flicked through a few more shots. "Wait a minute," he said. He turned the phone around. "Jazz, check out how puffy you look in this one."

She glanced up and saw Phoenix holding out the photo of her from the laundry. "Seriously? You're choosing now to pick on how I look? Real helpful, thanks, Phoenix." She shook her head. Was he ever going to take this investigation seriously? She checked the clock. **1:30 PM**. They needed to gather all the evidence they could, and already more than a quarter of the first **48 HOURS** had ticked away.

"No, I mean because of what you're wearing—the personal protective equipment," said Phoenix. "What if the kidnapper was wearing some kind of forensic suit and thick gloves? That would explain the fingerprint and the bloated leg."

Jazz's look of anger changed to joy. "Phoenix, that's brilliant!" She turned back to her app and added to the notes against the fingerprint shot:

Jazz felt an edgy anxiety running through her veins, ramped up by her excitement at working out this clue. "Let's not waste any more time," she said. "Phoenix, you get the tire print into the Treadmate app and start searching for a match on the boot print. I'm going to look at a major piece of evidence we haven't even started with yet."

"What's that?" he asked. He seemed grumpy that Jazz was telling him what to do.

"Anika's blog. It could hold the key to this whole investigation!"

34:25

Jazz clicked on the link from one of Anika's Facebook posts. Finally, here it was—Anika's blog. She had called it: *The Secret Diary: Days of Fear.*

As the website loaded up, Jazz felt annoyed with herself again for being so stubborn over the blog. The journal was missing and so was her best friend. Tears blurred her sight. Reading the blog was more important now than Anika could ever have imagined. It was possible that it held clues which could lead them to find her kidnapper.

Jazz knew Mack had definitely read most of the blog, and could give her a basic idea of what was in it. But the journal Anika had been blogging was important to the kidnapper for some reason, so Jazz wanted to take a thorough look at what it said for herself.

While Phoenix searched doggedly through images of boot prints, Jazz took a deep breath and focused as she started reading the first post.

13 October 1994
Today is the day I realized my husband is trying to kill me. I just stopped writing and looked at that sentence. Seeing the words on the page is almost more shocking to me than the realization itself. I've been suspicious for a while. Been feeling out of sorts. At first I thought it was homesickness after we moved. I missed our previous home and haven't made a lot of friends here. My sister did what she could, sending care packages with some of my favorite foods. I wouldn't have made it through those first few months without those chocolates that Karen sent. But the homesickness didn't get better. It got worse. And now it's become a real sickness, something that keeps me stuck in bed, too weak even to walk. I have no evidence of what my husband is doing, no proof. In fact, anyone who saw him fussing around me—checking to see if I've taken my medication, asking

if I want any more of the chicken soup that
he makes for me—would think how lucky I
am to have such a kind and loving husband.
And sometimes I think I am very lucky. And
I wonder if these thoughts about him trying
to kill me are part of my illness. Am I going
crazy? Perhaps the illness is in my brain and
I'm fearful and paranoid . . . Lately though,
I think I do sense a coldness in him. There's
something I can't put my finger on, something
not right, something that wasn't there before.
I overheard him on the phone to Karen and
he sounded so exasperated. They're both
pathologists, so normally their conversations
revolve around boring work stuff. But he
sounded really worked up. What else could that
have been about other than me, my sickness?
I suppose anyone would get tired of having
a sick partner after a while. We used to do
so many things together—hiking, traveling,
theater. Seeing films. But not anymore.
People talk about a "broken heart," but I feel
as if my heart has been stomped on—crushed.
I wish Karen was here. I need to tell someone!
And I need someone to tell me I'm just being

silly and of course everything's OK. That
Neil's not a murderer! That he does still love
me . . . that he could never . . . My thoughts
and feelings are so confused sometimes. I've
decided to keep this journal so that I have
something to work on, keep me occupied,
express these secret, terrible thoughts. And
hopefully it will just be some strange tale to
look back on if I ever get out of this mess . . .

No wonder Anika was so obsessed with the journal!
Jazz thought, looking up from the screen. She was
completely grabbed by the story. She glanced at the
comments on this first post, recognizing the handles
of lots of friends from school. The comments showed
they were just as compelled by the story, but she only
skimmed them, eager to head straight to the next post.

15 October
I'm ashamed now of what I wrote a couple
of days ago. Neil is truly the kindest, most
wonderful man, and I don't know how I could
have thought that he might be trying to kill
me. He must NEVER KNOW that I suspected
him. Luckily, I found a really good hiding

place for this journal. Karen is coming to visit and I'm sure once she arrives I'll feel a lot better. She and Neil can talk science. It's funny to remember now that I only met Neil because of Karen. They worked together in a lab. I used to pick her up and would often chat to Neil while I waited for her. That memory is so strange to me, both for how easy it used to be for me to get around, and the closeness Karen and I once shared. After Neil and I married she and I seemed to see less of each other. Our interests changed. We used to go out and do fun things together, but I started doing more and more of that with Neil and she retreated into her favorite hobby of tinkering around with computers. Although she lives so far away, this illness of mine seems to have brought my sister closer to me. I'll admit it's not only her companionship that I'm looking forward to. Maybe Karen will have some ideas about what it is that's afflicting me. Neil keeps pestering me to have more tests, but nothing is showing up on any of them to explain why I'm so weak and confused. I worry that Dr. Craven thinks that the illness

is all in my mind. If I told him of my earlier
(embarrassing) fears about Neil, he'd believe
I was truly crazy—especially if the next day I
told him that everything was all right and that
I was mistaken. He insists that my blood tests
are all normal. There's no sign of anything
amiss. And yet, day by day, I just know I'm
getting worse.

Jazz looked up from the screen, stunned by what she was reading. "This blog, Phoenix—it's kind of spooky. Riveting. I can't read it quickly enough!"

Phoenix was completely absorbed in what he was doing. He was scrolling through endless stock images of shoe soles on the left-hand side of a split screen. The right-hand split contained just one pattern—the image of the boot prints he had fixed and photographed in the disused laundry at the Belmonts'.

"Really," he said, not looking up. "What's it about?"

"This woman thinks her husband is trying to kill her," said Jazz.

Phoenix's head snapped up. "You mean we're on the hunt for a murderer?"

"Not necessarily," said Jazz. "She stays alive at least long enough to write plenty more entries. In this one she says how embarrassed she feels about being so suspicious of her husband."

Jazz refocused on the blogged entries from the unknown woman's journal. Part of what kept it so interesting was the way the mystery woman's mood kept changing. Some days she sounded desperate and suspicious; on other days the tone was much more hopeful.

24 October
I really feel I'm getting better. Perhaps it's because Karen is here. It's good to get to know my sister again. She seems very comfortable with Neil, ordering him around as if he were her own husband! I've even managed to eat some solid food again. Karen remembers many of my favorite dishes and spends ages in the kitchen preparing them. I can't believe that just a couple of weeks ago, I really thought Neil was trying to kill me! But I'll still keep hiding this journal, just in case. What would Neil think if he saw it?

Jazz paused in her reading. She was as engrossed as ever, but something didn't seem right. The unknown woman sounded so confused; was the journal trust-worthy? Or was it all in this woman's head? The thought of this woman's husband trying to kill her was awful to contemplate—part of her hoped the woman was deluded—but Jazz had to allow that Anika had been obsessed with this diary and someone had felt it worth stealing, and kidnapping Anika along with it. She needed to get to the end.

She clicked on "next post" and frowned. "That's odd," she muttered to herself and hit Refresh. The same thing happened. Rather than the next installment of Anika's blog, she kept getting an error.

"That can't be right!" Jazz cried. "The next post is missing!"

"Show me," demanded Phoenix, holding his hand out for the tablet. "It'll just be a bad link or something." He clicked through various links, but each time he got the same error message.

"It must be there," said Jazz. "That's the last post, the one that Anika put up the day she was—" she broke off.

"Coincidence?" said Phoenix, eyebrow raised. "I think not."

"You think the kidnapper has hacked her blog? Why would they do that?"

"You said this journal is about a woman whose husband killed her, right?"

"He was trying to. Without this last entry we don't know what happened."

"Well, maybe we don't need it to know at least part of the motive for the hack. Even attempted murder is serious stuff. Whoever did it must have thought they'd gotten away with it. But if the journal proved otherwise and someone published it online, for all the world to see—"

Phoenix paused. Jazz felt queasy as she started to realize what a horrible mess Anika had stumbled upon.

Then Phoenix voiced her worst thought. "If someone's going to this much effort, there must be something serious to hide."

33:30

Jazz and Phoenix stared at each other across the table. Neither knew what to say. Anika was in far graver danger than she could ever have realized when she innocently started blogging the journal.

The silence was broken by a ping from Phoenix's laptop.

"It's the Treadmate program," he said, glancing down at the screen. "We've got a match for the tire tread." He turned the screen to face Jazz.

On the left-hand side of the split screen she saw a promo image of a tire with a distinctive, asymmetrical tread—a zigzag alternating with a simpler diagonal pattern, running in rings around the circumference of the tire. The program identified it as a Suregrip SF 430B. On the right was the photograph of the tire print they had discovered in the soft earth near Deepwater. Although less clearly delineated, there was no disputing the fact that the tread pattern of both tires was identical.

TREADMATE

Match found: Suregrip SF 430B

"This is like a tire's fingerprint," said Phoenix. "If we can find a green SUV with these tires on it . . . plus the scrape marks that we can prove were caused by the gate at Deepwater . . . then we know we have the exact vehicle."

Jazz was still shaken by what the blog had revealed, but as they gathered more evidence she felt they were getting somewhere.

"I've got a match on the boot print too," Phoenix said,

turning the laptop back and switching to a different window. He turned the screen to face Jazz again.

"Here it is. Our kidnapper wears a size twelve Hardy-wear work boot. And we'll have no trouble identifying the actual boot because there's some damage in the kidnapper's print—see? The sole's been nicked a couple of times on the right-hand edge."

She glanced again at the time on her phone. **2:39 PM**. They were making progress but time still ticked away.

The thought of her best friend being taken and held prisoner by a cold-hearted killer overwhelmed her again. Jazz closed her eyes and imagined Anika could hear her thoughts: *We're coming to get you, Anika. Stay strong.*

"Here's what I still don't get," Phoenix said, interrupting her contemplation. "Taking the evidence—the journal—I can understand, but why did the intruder take Anika as well?"

"The jewelry box, remember?" said Jazz. "Maybe your crazy theory was right after all. Maybe there is something in that box that the kidnapper desperately needs to get hold of. And maybe it's not jewelry. Maybe it's a clue."

"But what clue?"

Jazz jiggled on her feet, energized by this new lead.

"We don't know yet. But we know the Belmonts are doing everything they can to find it. So while they work on that, we need to keep tracking down this kidnapper. I'll update our evidence," she said as she opened up CrimeSeen.

She navigated to the pictures of the tire tread and boot print and added in what they'd found out.

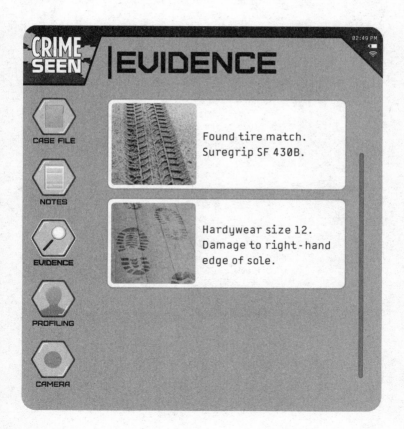

She started a new entry in Notes, titled "Journal,"
and added to the notes under "Kidnapper."

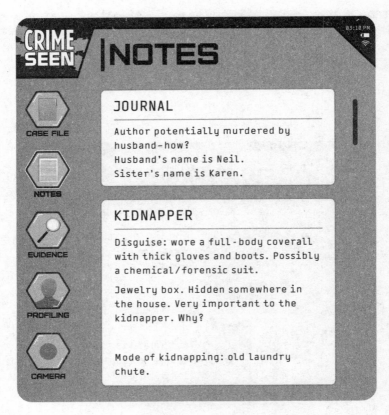

03:10 PM

JOURNAL

Author potentially murdered by
husband—how?
Husband's name is Neil.
Sister's name is Karen.

KIDNAPPER

Disguise: wore a full-body coverall
with thick gloves and boots. Possibly
a chemical/forensic suit.

Jewelry box. Hidden somewhere in
the house. Very important to the
kidnapper. Why?

Mode of kidnapping: old laundry
chute.

CASE FILE

NOTES

EVIDENCE

PROFILING

CAMERA

She stopped, arms folded, thinking about what to do
next.

"Do you remember, Phoenix, when I said someone
who'd be really familiar with the Belmonts' house would
be a former occupant? What about the previous owner?"

"How long have the Belmonts lived there?"

"All Anika's life. We need to find out who lived in that house before them."

She opened up a new window and typed in the Belmonts' address. The search returned a map graphic and lots of real estate sites, but they didn't give any details.

"I'm not getting anywhere with this web search."

"Why don't we ask Anika's folks?"

Jazz shook her head. "I don't want them more worried than they already are. Someone in the area is bound to know something. It's time for the personal approach—ready for some door knocking?"

32:20

"So what's our plan?" asked Phoenix, as they turned into Anika's street. "I'm guessing we're not just going to walk up and say, 'There's been a kidnapping, tell us what you know!'"

"Definitely not," agreed Jazz. "Especially since I promised Mr. Belmont I wouldn't tell anyone about the kidnapping. We don't want anyone getting scared and calling the police."

"Although a direct approach might get us more answers," Phoenix argued.

Jazz shook her head. "Another of the finer points of investigation you've yet to learn. It's called 'indirect interrogation.' We need a cover story. Real undercover police officers have to learn a whole script. We don't have to go that far, but we do need a plausible reason for our questions. Let's say we're researching the area for a school project."

"You call it indirect interrogation," said Phoenix. "I call it the nerd approach."

"Well, whatever you call it, I'll do the knocking," said Jazz. "And ask the questions."

"Why? Do you think I'll scare people off?"

Jazz raised an eyebrow. "You're not exactly a people person. And you frown a lot."

"Fine. Be my guest." Phoenix shrugged.

They began at the far end of the street from the Belmonts' and Deepwater, just in case the security guard was hanging around. Phoenix waited by the first home's wrought iron fence, and watched as Jazz strode confidently past the rosebushes that grew on either side of the walkway. She knocked loudly on the door, already running through the questions she was going to ask in her head. No one answered. She knocked again and waited, uncertainly, highly aware of Phoenix's watchful eyes on her. Time passed and, conceding defeat, she turned and headed back to where Phoenix stood on the sidewalk.

"Great start," he said.

At the next house, Jazz couldn't even open the front gate before two giant Rottweilers appeared, snapping and snarling. "Any chance you're a dog whisperer?" she asked Phoenix.

"I'm keen to help, but I'm not losing an arm for it."

Jazz was relieved that no dogs accosted her as she started up the walkway to the third house. Her knock, however, set off a volley of shouting from inside.

"Go away! We don't want whatever you're selling!"

She turned back to Phoenix, who was smirking by the gate. "Don't look at me," he said. "You're the people person, remember."

Jazz came back to the sidewalk, her earlier enthusiasm dissipating. She checked her watch—**4:00 PM**. Of the first **48 HOURS**, only thirty-two were left. Time was running out to gather useful evidence.

"How are we going to find out anything about the people who used to live at the Belmonts' if no one will talk to us?" Jazz wondered aloud.

They were already at the last house on the Belmonts' side of the street—the neighboring Victorian cottage. Summoning what hope she had left, Jazz walked up to it and knocked on the door.

A woman opened the door, dressed head to toe in shades of apricot, right down to her shoes and socks.

Before the woman could say a word, Jazz launched into her script. "Hello, my name is Jazz and I'm doing a report on the local area for a school project."

"I'm sure I'll be able to help you."

Jazz was braced for the woman to tell her to get lost, so it took a moment for her to register what she had said. "Really?"

"Yes, I've lived on this street for years! Debbie Chandler," she said, holding out her hand.

"I'm Jazmine and this is Phoenix," said Jazz, gesturing as Phoenix came hurrying up. "What do you know about that house?" she asked, indicating the Belmonts' with a nod of her head.

Debbie's chirpy smile changed to a look of concern. "Oh, that house seems to attract very bad karma." She paused, lowering her voice. "You know there was a murder there years ago?"

Jazz and Phoenix glanced quickly at each other. At last, they were getting somewhere! This talkative woman could be very helpful. But they had to play it just right . . .

"A murder?" Phoenix asked, eyes wide.

"Oh no!" Jazz played along. "That's awful!"

Debbie smoothed her hair and nodded. "Well, I think so. Even if nobody else did."

"What happened?" Jazz asked.

"A nice young couple used to live there, Linda and

Neil Sinclair. Linda was very sweet but quiet. She always seemed a little fragile, but then she became very ill indeed. Her sister had to come all the way from Redcliffe to help nurse her. I got to be quite good friends with Karen and she told me all about him—" her eyes flashed.

"Him?" asked Phoenix. "Who do you mean?"

Debbie lowered her voice conspiratorially. "Why the husband, of course. Karen was always very civil to Neil, but she didn't have a high opinion of him. And his actions after his wife's tragic death did seem odd. He just up and left. Had movers come later to take all their stuff away. Now why would a man leave like that, days after his wife died, if he didn't have a guilty conscience? Some neighbors said it was grief, but they didn't know Karen the way I did. And I can tell you from what I heard, the truth is he couldn't stand looking at the place where he had murdered his wife!"

"Oh, that's terrible. Do you know where he went?" asked Jazz, managing to keep her excitement out of her voice.

"He's in Sunshine Beach now. Living in some fancy place that he probably bought with her life insurance."

"Life insurance?" asked Phoenix.

"Oh yes. Two million dollars! That's what I heard."

"How shocking," said Jazz, genuinely horrified. "Why

didn't the police investigate? Surely they found out that he would gain from the insurance policy!"

"They might have made some enquiries," Debbie sniffed, "but that's about all they did. They might even have had reason to suspect him. But there was not enough evidence of foul play. Just poor Karen's word."

"Where's the sister now?" asked Jazz, all pretense about the school project forgotten.

"We lost touch," Debbie said sadly. She seemed almost in a reverie, staring into the distance as she remembered. "I only saw her again once, soon after Linda died—I was the one who had to break it to her that Neil was gone, that he had changed the locks and everything. I haven't seen either of them since." She snapped back to attention and narrowed her eyes at Jazz and Phoenix.

"I'm not sure how much this has to do with local history though." Before Jazz could think of an excuse, Debbie glanced at her watch and exclaimed, "Is that the time? I'm missing my favorite quiz show on TV. Lovely to talk to you!" And with that she closed the door, leaving Jazz and Phoenix standing on the porch, stunned into speechlessness.

They turned and walked down the sidewalk, past the Belmonts', scooted quickly by Deepwater and around the corner before turning to each other with excitement.

"So it was a murder!" breathed Jazz.

"With a huge payout for a motive!" replied Phoenix.

"And we've got their names." Jazz already had her phone out and was running a new search: Neil and Linda Sinclair . "I've got a hit!" she cried. "It's an article from a local newspaper."

26 November 1994

DEATH OF LOCAL WOMAN TRAGIC BUT NOT SUSPICIOUS

Tributes have flooded in from the local community following the death of Linda Sinclair, following a long illness.

"She and Neil were a lovely couple," neighbor Pat Perkins told *The Advertiser*. "Neil seemed quite devoted to her."

"I am of course devastated and bewildered by Linda's death," Mr. Sinclair said. "If only we'd been able to work out what was wrong, perhaps she'd still be with us." Mrs. Sinclair's physician, Dr. Craven, confirmed it was one of the most mysterious cases he had worked on. "For a young woman to change so dramatically from an active person to one confined to bed—it's as upsetting as it is confusing."

Locals also paid tribute to Mrs. Sinclair's sister, Karen Taylor, who had provided comfort and assistance to Mrs. Sinclair in her final days. Ms. Taylor was unavailable for comment.

Jazz added some notes to CrimeSeen.

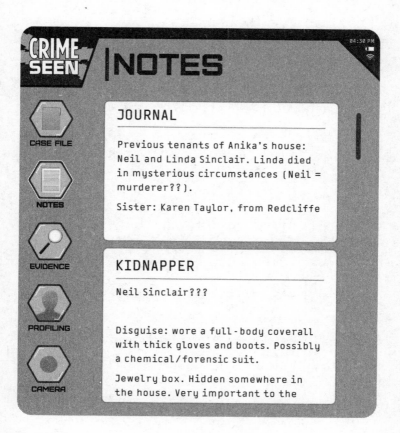

CRIME SEEN | NOTES   04:30 PM

CASE FILE
NOTES
EVIDENCE
PROFILING
CAMERA

JOURNAL

Previous tenants of Anika's house: Neil and Linda Sinclair. Linda died in mysterious circumstances (Neil = murderer??).

Sister: Karen Taylor, from Redcliffe

KIDNAPPER

Neil Sinclair???

Disguise: wore a full-body coverall with thick gloves and boots. Possibly a chemical/forensic suit.

Jewelry box. Hidden somewhere in the house. Very important to the

"We're really getting somewhere, Phoenix!" cried Jazz, her energy flooding back.

"I'm checking the phone directory," he said, sounding just as excited. "Oh," he said.

"What is it?"

"There are several Sinclairs listed in Sunshine Beach, but none with the initial 'N,'" he said, showing Jazz the list.

"Doesn't matter, it's still a great lead." Nothing was going to dampen her enthusiasm. "Next, we need to do a search on Ka—"

She was cut off by her phone ringing. "It's Mack," she said, taking the call. "Hi!"

"How's the investigation going?" Mack asked.

"Great, we're getting lots of leads."

"We? You mean, you and Phoenix?"

"Yeah, he's like, helping out and stuff."

Phoenix looked up from his phone. "Bit more than helping, don't you think?"

Embarrassed, Jazz turned away. "Can we meet? I'm dying to talk to you about Anika's blog."

"That's what I'm calling about," said Mack. "Can I come to your place? There's something I think you need to see!"

30:59

Phoenix headed home, muttering something about a list of chores. Jazz hurried to her house, eager to meet up with Mack. Her mother was on the phone and hung up as she walked in.

"Jazmine, I was just about to call you. I've been so worried. I thought something might have happened to you! I got home and you weren't here and there was no note or anything." Her mother's face was tight with anger and concern.

"Oh, Mum!" Jazz cried. "Don't be angry. I'm here and I'm safe!"

Her mother's face softened and Jazz ran and threw her arms around her. "Oh, Jazz. What's that about? I'm not complaining, of course!" her mum said, hurriedly.

Jazz kept her lips pressed tight together.

Her mum pulled away from the hug and glanced at the clock as she composed herself. "Where have you been anyway? You should have been home from school an hour ago."

Jazz was starting to squirm. No way could she tell her mother that she hadn't gone to school at all that day, let alone what she and Phoenix had been up to! But one thing her mother insisted on with her and Tim was a relationship of truth and trust. Jazz hated having to lie. Her mind racing to come up with a cover story, she started to speak when . . .

Ding-dong.

"That'll be Mack!" Jazz said with relief. "We're working on a project together!" *At least that's not a total lie*, she thought to herself as she ran to the front door. "Your timing is excellent," she said, hustling Mack straight upstairs to her room.

Once there, she opened up CrimeSeen and took Mack through what they'd found out so far.

"Sounds like you and Phoenix make quite the team," teased Mack.

"You mean me, Phoenix and his ego," said Jazz, filling Mack in on how Phoenix had lied about the DNA analysis machine.

"But you've found out so much stuff anyway. And

I've got something to add!" She grabbed the tablet and loaded up Anika's blog.

"I've already read through the posts," complained Jazz. "Unless you've found the one that was deleted?"

"No, and I'm kicking myself for not reading it earlier," replied Mack. "But it's not the posts I'm talking about. It's the comments." Mack clicked on the first post and scrolled down to the comments.

Most of the comments were very short, with a few words or emoji.

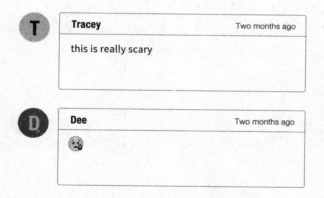

"But look at this one," Mack said. "It's different from the others."

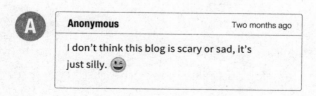

She clicked to the next post and down to the comments again. They were all short, but the one Mack pointed out had a very different tone than the others. It was just one word:

Jazz looked at Mack. "What's a narcissist? I know it's not exactly a compliment."

"I think it's someone who's up themselves. It's from a Greek legend about a guy who fell in love with his own reflection."

"And who are they accusing? Anika or Linda?" Jazz frowned. "Are there more?"

"Yup," said Mack, clicking through to a more recent post.

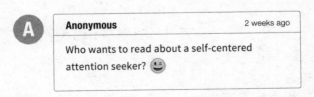

"They're all from an anonymous user, and they all have that winking smiley face at the end," Jazz observed.

"They get weirder," said Mack. "Check this one out."

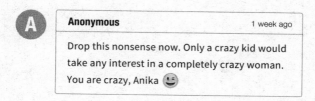

Anonymous   1 week ago

Drop this nonsense now. Only a crazy kid would
take any interest in a completely crazy woman.
You are crazy, Anika 😃

"Is that a threat?" Jazz asked.

"It's like Anonymous is attacking Anika for blogging the journal," Mack agreed. "Maybe trying to discredit her?"

Jazz got up to grab a copy of *Dark Places: Criminal Minds* from her bookshelf. "Let's check out what this has to say about narcissism." She flicked through it, then read out:

"Narcissists generally reveal a sense of entitlement, no empathy for others' feelings, and show an inflated sense of self-importance. They often have a dangerous and demanding character which is masked by superficial charm."

She looked up from reading to find Mack watching her with a twitching smile. "Remind you of anyone?" she asked.

"There should be a picture of Phoenix next to this description! Seriously though, a narcissist sounds like exactly the sort of person who could take a daughter from her parents' house without any worries."

"And leave smiley faces on threatening blog comments," said Mack.

Jazz clicked back into CrimeSeen and under the Kidnapper heading added:

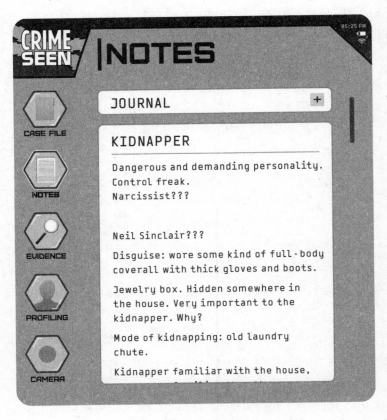

Thinking out loud, she continued, "This isn't about

personal gain. They haven't even demanded any money, just that jewelry box. It's all about them and covering their tracks."

"Maybe it's someone famous," offered Mack. "Someone who's already got lots of money, and wants to suppress the evidence to avoid a scandal."

She started searching `sinclair + celebrity`. "I'm not getting anything."

"The sister!" cried Jazz. "You've reminded me that I meant to run a search on her." She quickly typed `karen taylor`. "Oh no. There's a heap of them."

"Try adding 'Redcliffe.' Your notes mention that's where Debbie said she had come from."

"Oh, yes! Here's a Karen Taylor—and her business address is Redcliffe!"

Mack leaned in closer. "But that's a natural therapies place! Can't be her. She's a pathologist."

"That's disappointing," Jazz said. None of the other Karen Taylors looked promising at all.

Mack sighed. "Whatever happened to Linda Sinclair, I just hope we can find Anika."

"Me too," said Jazz softly.

Mack's phone beeped. "I have to go," she said, switching off her alarm and standing up.

"That's fine," Jazz said, giving her friend a reassuring

hug. "Go look after your family. This blog stuff has been a great help. I'll keep you posted."

Once Mack had left, Jazz was about to turn back to CrimeSeen when her phone whistled a message alert. She read it and gasped.

> I can tell you everything you need to know.
> Meet me at Deepwater tonight at 9 p.m.
> I must not be seen. Tell no one where
> you're going. I am in great danger.
> Linda Sinclair.

30:25

"What?" Phoenix's shocked question spoke for both of them. Jazz had called him as soon as she received the impossible message. "I don't believe it. Read it to me again."

"Trust me. The message is from Linda Sinclair," Jazz said for the third time.

"How could she possibly have your number?" Phoenix asked, bewildered.

"Never mind how she got my number, how is she messaging me at all? Is she still alive?"

Jazz and Phoenix were silent, in complete incomprehension. Finally, Phoenix spoke. "Maybe she faked her death after all, because she was really frightened and she's been in hiding."

"For what, like, twenty years?" Jazz's voice was

incredulous. "What if it's not her but someone using her name?"

"And how could that person know that we've even heard of Linda Sinclair?"

Once again, they were stumped, until almost at the same moment they arrived at a terrifying possibility.

Jazz said, "Unless it's not her at all but somebody pretending to be her to get us off the track!"

At the same time Phoenix said, "What if it's the kidnapper?"

"What should we do?" Jazz asked after a pause.

"Not sure. We could just ignore it."

"But if it really is Linda Sinclair, and we don't go and meet her, and something dreadful happens, how would we ever forgive ourselves?" Jazz asked.

"I think we have to agree to the meeting. Text her back and say we'll be there."

Jazz nodded to herself, pleased that she and Phoenix were thinking the same way.

"Had Mack read the blog? What did she say?" he asked.

Jazz filled him in on what Mack had revealed about the comments on Anika's blog. From the keyboard taps and mouse clicks coming through the phone, she knew he was looking them up for himself.

"Very interesting," he remarked. "Although that emoji seems weird on such a serious message. So after dinner tonight, I'll come by your place and we'll head to Deepwater early. We should do some surveillance first."

"And just how do you plan to do that? What if the security guy is there?"

"I've got just the thing," he replied, with an unmistakable grin in his voice.

* * *

It showed **8:09 PM** on his phone when, later that same evening, Phoenix walked downstairs with the bulging sports bag under one arm. He was heading for the front door when he heard his mother calling him. He groaned. Why was she choosing now to be interested in what he was doing?

She was sitting at the dining room table with a pile of papers in front of her.

"Phoenix," Dr. Lyons said, taking off her glasses. "It's hard to catch you these days. We need to have a chat."

"I'm just on my way out, Mum."

"I can see that. 'Out' seems to be where you're always going. I thought we agreed you would have an increased level of responsibility around the house while you're suspended."

"I'll do the dishes tomorrow, I promise."

"To be honest, Phoenix, I'd prefer you to be back at school rather than doing the dishes. Have you written that letter of apology yet?"

Phoenix didn't answer.

"You haven't, have you?" Dr. Lyons sighed. "Of course, I can't force you; there would be no point in that. But it's clear that you can't go on like this."

"But if I apologize it means everyone's missing the point. Their system needs to be more secure. They need to build a serious firewall and mitigation scripts—"

"You're still defending your position, I see. I really hope you have a change of attitude soon. So does your father. I've got some interesting cases coming up and I could use the help in the lab, but I'll be sticking with my rule. Until that letter is written, you're not to go in there." She put her glasses back on and returned to her paperwork.

27:30

Phoenix was so lost in his thoughts as he walked that he almost didn't spot Jazz waving at him from the shadows on the sidewalk outside Deepwater.

"What's in the bag?" she asked.

He opened it up to reveal a drone. Shaped like a large black *X*, with a rotor blade at the end of each arm, and a curved beaky scoop underneath each of the four arms, it reminded Jazz of a very large clawed spider.

"It's against the law to use it in a built-up area. But I think if we're after a killer, we might have to bend the rules a bit."

"Anything that gives us a better idea of what's lying in wait before we go in sounds good to me," said Jazz. She looked up at the dense outline of Deepwater and shuddered. It had never felt so sinister. Now it seemed to loom over Anika's house. She remembered reading about a killer who used to watch his victims' houses for days before he attacked, getting acquainted with the daily rhythm of his targets—what time they left the house, what time they came home from work, when they locked up the house, when they went to bed . . . The kidnapper could have done that to make sure that all was quiet the night they took Anika.

Crouching where they were hidden by the stone pillars at the gate, Phoenix placed the drone on a level part of the driveway.

He opened the control app on his phone and started the ignition. The four rotors started spinning, gaining speed until they were an almost invisible blur. A red diode gleamed, highlighting the inner parts of the drone's four arms. The slight whine increased and as Phoenix guided his finger upward on the screen, the black drone lifted off the ground and over the front yard toward the house.

"But it won't be able to see anything," Jazz said, looking at the black fuzz on Phoenix's screen.

"Watch this," he whispered.

Phoenix changed a setting and suddenly the drone transmitted a clear black-and-white picture.

"Infrared?" Jazz asked.

"Correct."

They both watched intently as Phoenix steered the small craft past each window of Deepwater's upper story, letting it linger a moment. Nothing moved inside. Only the grayish feedback of empty, derelict rooms, one with an old chair leaning against a wall, and the occasional running white form of a rat skipping across the floor.

After they'd checked out the upper floors, they used the drone on the windows of the ground floor, moving it around the outside of the old mansion.

"Looks safe enough," said Phoenix as he brought the drone back to where they crouched. Once it had landed and the rotors wound down, he stowed it back in his bag.

Keeping low, they made their stealthy way up the driveway. Even though they'd been there earlier that day, things looked very different in the dark. Now the overgrown grounds had a menacing feel. Strange sounds in the undergrowth made Jazz think of snakes and deadly spiders, or bats that might suddenly attack her head. Long brambly branches with vines weaving them together seemed to have grown since their visit only hours ago, and almost blocked their way.

They ducked and pushed their way through the foliage and finally reached the overgrown terrace.

Once a place for elegant lunches and afternoon teas, it was now a derelict space, infested with weeds and grass coming up between the stone flags.

"Where do you think we're supposed to meet her?" Jazz whispered.

Using only starlight and their night-sensitive eyes, the two investigators crept along the terrace to the front entrance. The huge front door stood ominously ajar.

The thought of going in was not at all appealing. Jazz took a deep breath. There were some things about being a hands-on investigator that were much more fun to just read about. But no way in the world was she going to admit that to Phoenix.

"Let's go in," she said.

They stepped inside and waited until their eyes had adjusted to the even-darker space inside the tumbledown old mansion. The beams of their phones slid across the walls and ceiling, showing them that once, maybe a century and a half ago, Deepwater would have been a glorious dwelling. They were standing in what would have been a large reception room, the marble fireplaces long removed. The outline of a huge mirror or painting still showed over the mantelpiece. Stained wallpaper showed signs of its original beauty in its pattern of garlanded rose wreaths and ribbons. The ceiling, collapsed in one corner, had been decorated with tiny cherubs. The floorboards creaked beneath their feet as Jazz and Phoenix crept along the main corridor.

"Let's check in all these downstairs rooms first," whispered Phoenix, a little intimidated by the size of the decaying mansion and the stench of damp and rot. They tiptoed from room to room only to find more decay and damp, but there was no sign of Linda Sinclair.

"Upstairs it is," said Jazz, eyeing the semi-spiral staircase, "though that staircase looks pretty dodgy. I think we should stick to the sides of the steps and not put too much weight in the middle."

Cautiously, following the narrow beams of light from their phones, they moved up the once-grand curving staircase until they came to the landing, a long gallery with rooms on either side. They headed for the first room on the western side, pushing open the heavy door. Phoenix entered first. He freaked as bats, spooked by the light from the phone, squeaked past his head.

"Harden up, Phoenix," Jazz said, then froze as she saw Phoenix staring at her. "What is it?" she asked, trying not to sound panicked. "Is one stuck in my hair?"

"Not *your* hair," said Phoenix. "Bat hair!" He ran a quick image search on his phone. "That's what those hairs were that we found in Anika's room."

"You think Anika is here?"

Phoenix shook his head. "Doubt it."

"But whoever took her has been here," Jazz said, looking behind her. "Or might still be?"

Something scurried across the floorboards as they headed to the next room. "Rats! Even worse! What's next?"

"With all this animal life I think we can assume there's no one—" Phoenix broke off.

"What is it?" whispered Jazz. "Do you see someone?"

Phoenix shook his head and pointed his flashlight at the floor. A set of footprints gleamed in the dust. Trailing them with the flashlight, the prints led along the floorboards of the empty room and over to the window. Discarded candy wrappers littered the floor near the window and Jazz bent down and picked one up.

"Cherry de Lix," she said, showing Phoenix the wrapper.

Phoenix shook his head. "Never heard of them."

"Look," Jazz whispered. She was peering out into the darkness past the dusty windowpane with its coating of spiderwebs and dead insects. "This window looks right down onto the Belmont house. If the lights were on we'd be able to see inside their living room through that huge window."

"The kidnapper's observation post," said Phoenix. A sound made them swing around from the window. "What was that? Linda?"

Together, they hurried out of the upstairs room and crept along the wide hallway, straining to listen, trying to discover where the sound had come from. The crunch of footsteps reached them from outside.

"Quick!" said Jazz. "Back downstairs!"

As fast as they dared, they stumbled down the crumbling staircase. They stopped at the bottom, listening carefully. Jazz was about to point to something on the ceiling when they heard the footsteps, crunching much more clearly, from the back of the house.

"This way," said Phoenix, darting into the corridor. "She must be in the backyard." Barely breaking stride, he flung open the back door and bolted out. Jazz heard a strangled cry as Phoenix disappeared from view!

"Phoenix!" cried Jazz. Creeping forward, she saw a yawning hole in the ground with steps leading down. A cellar! "Are you OK?" Jazz heard nothing but some muffled groans. "I'm coming down." Jazz picked her way down the stairs.

"I'm fine," said Phoenix, taking Jazz's hand as she helped him up off the floor. "More shocked than bruised. You didn't need to come all the way down—"

BANG!

The meager light that had drifted down into the cellar was suddenly shut out. The sound of a bolt scraping home confirmed their worst fears. Someone had blocked off the cellar opening.

They were trapped!

26:57

Phoenix clambered up the stone steps and started banging on the covering. "Hey, open up!" he cried. "Let us out!"

"Oh, genius idea, Phoenix," said Jazz. "I'm sure whoever just locked us in here is going to turn around straightaway and let us out."

"Got a better idea?"

"Yes, hello?" said Jazz, waving her phone. "I'll just call for help." She frowned at her screen. "Oh no! There's no signal."

"These walls are concrete and probably three feet thick," said Phoenix, checking his phone as well. "It's these old houses!"

"We've gotta get rid of this cover," said Jazz, shining the light from her phone to reveal a timber lid across the hole above the stairs. "Everything else in this place is rotting. We should be able to lift it."

Jazz got into position on the stair beside Phoenix. The two of them raised their bent arms until they had the palms of their hands flat on the underside of the timber cover.

"On the count of three, push as hard as you can. Put everything into it, OK?" Phoenix said.

"You bet."

"One, two, three—push!"

Jazz pushed with all her might. "Ouch!" she cried. "My wrist!" She shook it out and rubbed it for a moment, then said, "That's better. But the lid didn't budge!" She put her mouth near the cover and shouted, "Help! Somebody! Anybody! Help us!"

"Like you said, genius idea," said Phoenix. "Let's push again."

Still the cover did not move. Their combined efforts only resulted in rocks and stones falling from the housing.

"Ouch!" Jazz yelled, as a stone hit her on the head.

Over and over they tried, even taking turns on a higher step to push the cover with the strength of their backs. For the next hour they strained against the hatch, but it wouldn't budge.

Finally, Phoenix dropped down and sat, dejected and in darkness, on the steps. "This isn't working," he said. "We've got to think of something else. What if no one comes close to this cellar for days?"

"We're not going to be able to help Anika!" Jazz bit her lip, refusing to give in to the tears that threatened. The darkness of the cellar didn't help her feeling of hopelessness, but they were trying to conserve their phone batteries. A thought struck. "The cameras!"

"What cameras?" asked Phoenix, wearily.

"You didn't notice the security camera above the back door?"

"No!" He paused. "Why is that a good thing?"

"Maybe security will see us and come and rescue us."

"Arrest us for trespassing more likely."

Jazz leaned back in exhaustion against the unyielding hard stone that walled the cellar. She didn't want to be arrested, but the alternative was far worse. What if nobody ever came? What if they were down here for days? They had no water. Nothing to eat.

A stone hit her hard on the head and she felt like screaming in frustration and fear. "There can't be many more stones left in the wall on each side of the steps. They all seem to have fallen on my head," she said bitterly.

"Brilliant!" cried Phoenix as he jumped up and hit his head on the cellar cover. "Jazz, you are brilliant! We should have thought of this earlier."

Jazz heard him go down the steps and start crawling around on the dirt-floored cellar.

"This oughta do it," he said.

"What are you talking about?"

"A tool," Phoenix said as he came back up the stairs wielding a rusty old pair of hedge clippers. "If we can use this to dislodge the stone housing around the timber—"

"I get it! We could loosen the cover!" Jazz blurted with excitement. "Let's do it!"

Phoenix was already in position back on the third step, but instead of banging at the cover, he started chiseling away at the join between the sandstone blocks which held the cover in place. When he tired, Jazz took over while he rested. When she needed a break, Phoenix took over again. It seemed to take forever but finally, the big stone block on the right-hand side underneath the timber cover started to move just a little when they pushed it. This gave both of them renewed vigor, and although their hands were sore and rubbed raw, they kept at it.

Now they could see a crack of dim moonlight which got wider and wider as the stone got looser and looser.

"I think we're just about there," said Phoenix. He gave one more shove, then yelled, "Look out!" as they flattened themselves against the wall. There was a huge crashing sound and the big stone block smashed its way down the steps, coming to a thudding halt at the bottom. Phoenix gave a hoot of triumph and squeezed his way out through the narrow hole. Jazz followed, pushing herself through and out into the refreshing night air.

"We did it! We're free!" she cheered. "Let's get outta here!"

24:54

Phoenix sat slumped on the curb, a few houses down from Deepwater, exhaustion and fear showing on his face. "That was close," he said.

"I think we're the ones getting too close," said Jazz. "It must have been the kidnapper who locked us in after luring us with that fake message from Linda Sinclair."

"There's something weird going on here," said Phoenix. "How did the person claiming to be Linda Sinclair get hold of your phone number to leave the phony text message?"

Their phones started pinging with messages they had missed while locked underground. Jazz checked the notifications. "Oops," she said guiltily. "My mum's been calling."

"No such luck for me," said Phoenix. "I wonder

sometimes if they'd notice if I didn't come home at all."

"If only!" said Jazz. "If my mum could legally put a tracking device on me, she would."

Phoenix stared at her.

"Um . . . are you OK?" she asked.

"Quick, what's Anika's blog address again?" he demanded.

"What are you doing?" Jazz asked as Phoenix logged on to Anika's blog site once more.

"A tracking device—those emojis. It's obvious."

"What are you talking about?"

Phoenix raced to the first of Anonymous's comments and tapped on the emoji. "See that?"

He copied the URL address to a text editor and Jazz leaned over to see.

```
ftp://58.106.230/45/images/trackme.png
```

"Oh no!" she whispered. "Is that what I think it is?"

"Jazz, that emoji isn't just a winking smiley face—it's a tracker! Whoever's running that tracker records everyone who logs on to this blog, and at the moment that's you and me. You know that every device connected to the internet is assigned a unique address? An IP address? Anonymous has been watching us all this time!"

Jazz's eyes widened at what Phoenix was saying.

"But how did Anonymous know to pay attention to us, and not the other online followers?"

"Jazz," he went on urgently, "when did you first look at Anika's blog of the journal?"

"Today, at the gym."

"And I first looked at it when you told me about those weird comments." Phoenix paused, his mind racing. "I know how they got onto us! So suddenly, Anonymous sees these two usernames appearing and all they're reading are the journal entries. They don't look at anything else, like Anika's stories. So, assuming Anonymous knows something about Anika's kidnapping, they might be wondering why we picked today to suddenly get so interested. Right away they've got our locations and it's just a matter of time before they find out our real names . . . and addresses."

A jolt of fear went through Jazz's body, shocking every cell. All this time they'd been trying to work out the identity of the killer, and the kidnapper, this evil person had been watching *them* as they logged on, gathering information about them, tracking them down.

"So are we saying that this Anonymous might know the kidnapper?" she whispered in horror.

"Either that or Anonymous could *be* the kidnapper," said Phoenix.

The night seemed to close more tightly around them. Jazz unclenched her fists, realizing that the fear had made her whole body tense. They both nearly jumped out of their skins when their stunned silence was suddenly shattered by Jazz's phone ringing. Puzzled by the unfamiliar number, she answered it with trembling fingers.

A horrible hissing voice filled her ears: "I know who you both are and I know where you and your families live. Back off. Both of you. You know I've killed before and I'll kill again—anyone who gets in my way. Anyone! Consider this the only warning you're going to get."

Phoenix, alerted by Jazz's shocked face, grabbed her phone and listened—but the line was dead. "What did they say?" Phoenix demanded.

Jazz repeated the words to him in a shaky voice.

"It was a warning, and a threat as well." Phoenix stood up. "Let's move." He kept talking as they walked, his voice less certain. "My dad always says, 'If you can walk away from a fight, do.' We're being threatened by the kidnapper who's possibly killed before. If we keep investigating, we could get hurt or make a mess of things and put Anika's life in even more danger."

"Do you think we should walk away now?" asked Jazz, half-disappointed, half-relieved at his words. They'd both done a lot of work so far. Maybe they should hand over what they knew to the proper authorities. But what if telling the police only put Anika in more danger?

"I prefer my boxing coach Simon's saying: 'If you can't walk away from a fight, take it on with everything you've got. Don't give up until the end—whatever that might be.'" Phoenix paused. "That's our choice."

"I'm scared," said Jazz, frightened further by his words, glancing around as they reached her house. A new and even more frightening realization hit her.

"Phoenix, even if we stop our investigation now that the killer knows we're onto them, do you really think they're going to leave us alone?"

Phoenix shook his head. "Whoever it is can't afford to let us stay around. We know too much. And they know we know too much." He lowered his voice. "We'll have to be eliminated."

Jazz raised her face to look at his, knowing that it would be like looking into a mirror—both of them pale with shock and terror. The sudden shrieking of a night bird made them both jump.

"They're going to come after us," she whispered, "so now we can't just give up. Even if we wanted to. Not if we want to survive."

"So we don't really have a choice at all," said Phoenix.

"We've got to give it everything we have. It's not only Anika's life that's on the line. It's ours too."

"What's your plan?" Jazz asked.

"We start with the kidnapper's own tracking device. Using it, we can track *them*! All I need is the right program. I'll do it as soon as I get home. This is great." Phoenix was visibly brightening as he spoke. "And the best bit is they won't be expecting us to come after them! They'll be thinking we've crawled back home to our families to hide."

"OK," Jazz said, feeling a little more hopeful. "We'll have to be really careful."

"Of course we'll be careful. Three people's lives depend on it."

* * *

Jazz snuck upstairs, relieved not to bump into her mother. *I could be in a lot of trouble tomorrow*, she thought, *but right now I've got to crash.*

Jazz's sleep wasn't restful, haunted by dreams of Anika and an unseen, hissing monster that had taken her friend in the night. Strange humanoid figures with animal features drifted through them. She kept waking up in fits of anxiety, worried she was trapped in the dark cellar again, before falling back into another restless doze.

The next time she woke up, her alarm clock said it was **4:00 AM**. More than half of the vital first **48 HOURS** had slipped away.

The thought that the kidnapper had been electronically following them all the time caused her to sit up suddenly in the darkness. The kidnapper knew where she lived. The kidnapper had come for Anika in the middle of the night. What if he came for her?

It wasn't until dawn brought relief from the dark, and the chirp of morning birds drove away the dreadful sounds she'd been imagining, that Jazz was able to fall back into a troubled sleep.

15:00

The chime of her phone woke Jazz later that morning. It was Phoenix, sounding excited.

"The tracker on the emoji worked! I've got an address in Sunshine Beach."

"Just like Debbie Chandler said!" exclaimed Jazz, instantly wide-awake.

"It matches one I looked up yesterday—C. Sinclair."

"But his initial isn't C. It's N."

"It's a Sinclair. We need to get out there and check the place out! Can you meet me at the gym in thirty minutes?"

Before Jazz could ask how they were going to get to Sunshine Beach, Phoenix was gone.

She headed downstairs for breakfast. Helping herself to some cereal in the empty kitchen, she felt a brief hope that her mother might have already gone out for the day, saving any awkward explanations.

"You got home late last night," said her mum, startling her as she appeared at the door of the kitchen. "I couldn't sleep a wink for worrying about you."

You're not the only one, thought Jazz.

"You don't seem to be taking my concerns very seriously. Don't you realize how important it is for me to know where you are, and preferably to know that you're safely here at home?"

Jazz decided against mentioning that Anika had been "safely at home" when she was kidnapped. She couldn't tell her mum and she felt awful about it still. But who knows who her mum might feel she had to tell, and if the police found out . . .

Her mother noticed Jazz's bag on the counter. "Where do you think you're going now?"

"I'm sorry about last night, Mum, but today's really important. I have to—"

"Have to what?" Her mother sighed. "Jazmine, please tell me you're not going out again. You've been running yourself ragged. Why don't you stay home and we can go to a movie this afternoon?"

There were so many things Jazz wanted to say, like the fact that her best friend was missing and no one else was doing the investigating so she had to. She hated lying to her mother, but to tell her the truth would have been to send her worry levels into overdrive. She knew she would also have to lie about her plans for the day.

"I need to go to Mack's. She's already having a tough time and she's pretty upset about Anika too." Jazz realized her mistake as soon as she spoke, but her mum unwittingly came to her rescue.

"Has Mack been dragged into this fight between you and Anika?"

Jazz nodded miserably.

"OK then, you can go," her mum relented. "But please try and sort this out sooner than later. You need to stick with your good friends in high school. It's not worth losing them over some silly project. And Jazz?"

"Yes, Mum?"

"Don't be back late!"

* * *

Jazz hurried over to Phoenix as soon as she arrived at Schmick n Fit. "So what's the plan?" she asked. "How do we get to Sunshine Beach from here?"

Phoenix nodded to where Simon was finishing up a session in the ring. "You heard what he said yesterday;

he's happy to help."

Jazz gave a doubtful frown. "We can't tell him any-thing about what we're doing, Phoenix."

"I know that," he said with an exasperated sigh. "Let me do the talking."

Simon smiled at them as they walked over. "Shall I leave these on?" he asked, indicating his boxing gloves.

"Actually I was thinking of a different kind of session today," replied Phoenix. "Fancy a trip to the beach?"

Simon looked from Jazz to Phoenix, confused. "What are you two up to?"

"It's all part of that, ah, homework we were doing here yesterday. We just need a ride. Unless, of course, you want to lend me your truck."

"Ha!" scoffed Simon. "No one's taking that baby out for a spin. Just give us a sec to cool off and I'll be right with you."

Phoenix gave Jazz a triumphant wink as he steered her toward the parking lot.

* * *

Jazz navigated as Simon drove. When they reached the right street, they slowed down, looking for street numbers.

"422, 418, 410—there, 406, that's it. Pull over down the street a bit."

They scoped the building as they drove past. It was a two-story house with a double garage beside it. This stood behind a chest-high stone fence lined with bushes to provide privacy.

"Pretty ritzy," Phoenix muttered.

"Do friends of yours live here?" asked Simon, eyeing the flashy street.

"Not a friend, exactly," said Phoenix.

"We're here to . . . pick something up," added Jazz.

Simon eyed them both. "I get the feeling you're not telling me everything."

"You wouldn't believe me if I did!" said Phoenix. "I'll catch you back at the gym," he added, opening the pickup's door and stepping out onto the sidewalk.

"Thanks for the lift," said Jazz, then she followed Phoenix out of the truck. They watched as it drove away, Simon giving a toot of the horn before turning the corner.

"Look," said Jazz, "there's a cafe right across the street from Sinclair's house. We can stake it out from there."

Phoenix gave a nod, but they hadn't even made it to the entrance when movement from across the road caught their eyes.

The garage door lifted completely to reveal a large vehicle nosing its way out.

Jazz gasped. "A green SUV!"

"And its passenger-side door is scratched! That's our guy! It's the kidnapper!" Phoenix said.

Jazz made to cross the road.

"Where are you going?" hissed Phoenix.

"Anika could be in there! We've got to get inside!" she called back.

As the car roared off, the automatic garage door started rumbling down. Phoenix made a split-second decision, then followed Jazz across the road. They raced up the driveway and ducked under the garage door just before it closed, the *thunk* echoing around the dimly lit space.

13:30

Inside the garage, they looked around at the shelves of tools and spare parts.

"Did you get a look at the driver?" Phoenix asked Jazz.

"No. Did you?"

Phoenix shook his head.

Jazz went over to a pair of work boots which stood along the wall near the front of the garage. She picked them up. "Yes! Size twelve Hardywear! Here, hold them so I can see the bottom of them," she said to Phoenix.

Jazz got out her tablet and opened up the CrimeSeen app, and compared the sole of the boots to the picture of the boot print they'd found in the Belmonts' laundry.

"You can see exactly the same damage to the sole," she confirmed. "It's a match!"

Phoenix was peering at the oil stains on the floor.

"I think we've got another match here," he said, holding his hand out for the tablet. He checked the tire print that he'd run through the Treadmate app. "Yep, zigzag pattern matches." Phoenix straightened up. "That's three important points—the green SUV with a scratch, matching work boots and tire tread," he continued. "That seems pretty conclusive."

"It's all circumstantial though," said Jazz. "Even so, it is pointing to Neil Sinclair as being our guy. It would help if we could find some hard evidence that links him directly to Anika."

Phoenix noticed a door in the back wall of the garage. "We've got to get inside the house."

Jazz could only nod. The thought that Anika could be here filled her with nervous excitement. She tried the handle. "It's locked." She looked around the shelves in the garage.

"Do you reckon we could pick the lock?" asked Phoenix. "Do you know how?"

Jazz rolled her eyes. "I wouldn't be standing here like a dork if I did." She picked up a long file with a pointed end. "We'll just have to go old school."

"Are you serious?" said Phoenix. "I hope the kidnapper doesn't come back while we're doing this," he muttered.

"I hope the kidnapper doesn't come back—" Jazz gave a grunt as she pushed the file between the doorjamb and the lock, "—at all," she said as the door frame splintered enough to release the lock.

Jazz tugged the internal door open, and cautiously, they crept inside the house. The first room they encountered was a narrow laundry. They tiptoed through it and came to a kitchen which opened out into a large living area.

"Let's just make sure there is no one else home," warned Phoenix. They stood in silence, listening. "I think we're clear."

A few business letters lay on the counter and Jazz glanced at the one on top addressed to Mr. Cornelius Sinclair. "Cornelius—Neil for short! That's why it was listed under C. Sinclair."

"And Jazz, look at this whiteboard."

> # TO DO
>
> ## Get respray quote for car. ;)

"There's a winking face next to it! Just like the emoji Anonymous left on Anika's blog." Jazz turned to

Phoenix. "Phoenix, I think this proves that Anonymous is the kidnapper, who is Neil Sinclair! Who could be a murderer too . . . and we're in his house. Let's see if we can find Anika quickly so we can get out of here!"

Stealthily, they searched the downstairs floor. As they opened each door Jazz's heart caught in her mouth, hoping to see Anika there but at the same time feeling terrified of what they might find. A thorough search of the rooms downstairs turned up nothing.

A glance out the door to the backyard showed an open expanse of lawn—nowhere to hide a hostage.

"How about we keep looking for Anika upstairs?" said Jazz, one hand on the banister.

Phoenix nodded. "And for more evidence."

Step by step, they crept upstairs until they came to the landing, furnished with a comfortable sitting nook. A tall storage closet with a sliding door was flanked on each side by bedrooms. Jazz pushed the door of the first room open and cautiously stepped inside.

It was a bedroom, clearly a man's, because of the shaving gear on the dressing table, and the pair of trousers draped over a chair. The bedclothes had been pulled up roughly but not made well. A framed wedding photo hung on the wall, showing a fit, radiantly happy couple, the man strongly built and with a slightly receding hairline.

"Do you think that's Sinclair?" Phoenix asked. "Maybe this is his second wife."

Jazz looked closer and gasped. "The photo's dated! It's from the nineties. If that's Sinclair, it must be him and Linda." She grimaced. "What kind of sicko keeps a photo of himself and the wife he murdered in his bedroom?" An answer from her true crime reading came to her almost immediately. "Killers often keep trophies!"

They checked the walk-in closet, the bathroom and under the bed, but found no further evidence of Anika.

"Let's try the next room," whispered Jazz.

The second bedroom also showed signs of habitation. "Is someone staying with him?" pondered Phoenix.

"This looks like a woman's bedroom," Jazz replied. A dress hung on the back of the door and a pair of high heels poked out from under the bed. "A woman with massive feet," commented Jazz, looking more closely at the shoes.

They stepped back out into the hall. "There's one more room," whispered Phoenix, nodding at the closed door that faced them at the end of the hall. Jazz turned the handle, heart pounding, then opened the door.

Her heart sank. This room was a sparsely furnished home office. There was nowhere for Anika to be hidden. Nevertheless, she scanned the bookshelves.

She stifled a gasp when she spotted a volume bound in red-and-white leather hiding in plain sight among the science textbooks. They may not have found Anika but now they had the evidence they needed—the journal! Jazz pulled it triumphantly from the shelf.

"Gotcha!" she said, showing it to Phoenix. "Linda Sinclair's journal is right here in Neil's house! It was taken from Anika's bedroom the night she disappeared. This clinches it."

Phoenix made a triumphant fist. "Yes! We've got him!"

12:58

"**W**e need to read that final post that was deleted from Anika's blog."

Jazz carefully flipped through the handwritten entries of the journal that filled page after page until she found one they hadn't read. She and Phoenix could scarcely breathe as they took it in.

22 November
I've been crying for days now because there is no longer any doubt about it. I've been doing research when he's not here and my symptoms point to the awful truth. Neil is definitely trying to kill me!
I'm getting weaker by the day and can barely get out of bed. Karen says I must go to the

police—and I will. I believe he is poisoning me in some way, probably putting it in my food or drinks. But if I don't eat anything, I'll get weaker and weaker until I starve. I'm in a terrible predicament. I pretend to eat the food he's brought me, and eat only what Karen brings me. Thank goodness for my sister, otherwise I'd starve to death or die of poisoning!

And finally, I have the proof I need. I needed evidence. And now I have it. I have hidden it safely in my wooden jewelry box. No one, not even Karen, knows where I've put it. With her help, I will get to the police, make a statement and hand the evidence over to them. Meanwhile, I mustn't arouse his suspicions. If he suspects that I know . . . he might do away with me on the spot! Within a few days, I should have my suspicions confirmed and then I'll be able to get him charged with attempted murder. I'll write more tomorrow as I'm feeling very weak today.

Another entry, dated the following day, the handwriting feeble and faint, was very short:

23 November 1994
Something happened. How could I have been so
wrong about the man I married . . . ?
LT

Jazz and Phoenix were both quiet for a moment.

"Linda was poisoned," Jazz said, looking at Phoenix, "by her husband. Neil Sinclair."

"And she had proof," nodded Phoenix, "hidden inside the jewelry box. Just as we thought. It's vital for Sinclair to find it because it proves he's a murderer."

"It's vital to us too. It's the direct evidence we need to nail this sicko." She glanced again at the final entries. "There's a clue too in the way she signed off—LT. That's what the kidnapper—Sinclair—said is on top of the jewelry box. It must stand for Linda Taylor, her name before she got married."

"Hey, what was the date on that newspaper article you found?" asked Phoenix.

Jazz grabbed her phone and opened up the link. She raised her eyes and gave Phoenix a somber look. "Three days after that entry."

"She didn't survive to write any more." Phoenix gave a sad shake of his head.

"I wonder what she meant when she wrote 'something

happened,'" pondered Jazz.

"No idea. Maybe we'll find out . . . and maybe we won't."

The edgy anxiety Jazz had been feeling the whole time they'd been in Sinclair's house escalated to a full-scale ringing in her ears as she fully realized the gravity of the story they were unraveling. And Anika was caught in the thick of it!

"This confirms it," said Phoenix. "Sinclair finds out about the blog and gets very, very worried. Especially when he reads that bit about the hidden evidence. He's got to get that jewelry box and that journal."

"But where is he holding Anika?"

"I'm going to check out the laptop," Phoenix said, moving over to Neil Sinclair's home office computer and giving the mouse a wiggle.

Brow knitted, Phoenix clicked and tapped between windows and applications. Jazz paced behind him, arms folded across her chest.

"Just as we thought," he said, directing Jazz's attention to the screen. For a moment, Jazz thought they were back in the Belmonts' house looking at the CCTV—it was the same gray, grainy style of footage. But this was showing the Belmonts' house from the outside, clearly from a second-story window.

"Deepwater," said Jazz.

"Yep," agreed Phoenix. "This file is just one in a folder full of surveillance feeds, all from the last few months."

Jazz looked at the dates on the surveillance files, then checked her notes about the blog on CrimeSeen. "The surveillance started just after Anika started blogging. He must have been watching Anika's house for ages." Jazz shivered. "Crouching up there in the dark, rotting mansion, waiting to swoop down and snatch Anika."

Phoenix clicked on some more files on the computer and let out a low whistle. "Sinclair really knows what he's doing."

"What do you mean?" asked Jazz.

"This," he said, bringing up a file filled with white lines of code against a dark background. "It's how he took down that last blog post. This is some serious hacking," Phoenix added.

"Are you admiring him?" said Jazz, incredulously. "This guy murdered his wife and has taken my best friend hostage. He's a—" Jazz stopped, unable to go on. What had happened to Anika? All through the investigation she had been spurred on by the thought of helping her, saving her, getting her back. *But what if* . . . she tried to stop herself finishing the thought. *What if Anika wasn't OK?*

Phoenix opened up yet another window. "What the—"
he gasped as he stepped back from the screen. "Jazz,"
he said, in a low voice that made her look up, fearful.
"You need to see this."

12:16

"**A**nika," Jazz breathed, tears flooding her eyes.

On-screen was grainy CCTV footage of Anika, huddled in a tiny room. The recording data running along the bottom of the screen showed this was live surveillance.

SATURDAY 11:44 AM

"Where is she?" cried Jazz. "Phoenix, do something!"

Before he could look any further, they heard the sound of a vehicle outside.

Phoenix jumped up and ran to the window. "It's Sinclair! He's just pulled back into the driveway!"

"If he goes in through the garage, he'll see the broken door lock!" cried Jazz. "We've got to get out of here—fast!"

Phoenix shook his head as he turned from the window. "He won't see . . . yet. He's heading for the front door. We have to hide!"

They hurried from the office. After a moment's hesitation, Phoenix made for the tall closet on the landing and slid open the door. Much of the closet was taken up with shelves piled neatly with towels and sheets. But there was also an area for hanging coats that provided the possibility of a hiding spot—as long as no one opened the door! Jazz and Phoenix stepped inside and pulled the door across in front of them. They tried to calm their breathing in the pitch dark as they heard the front door opening and Sinclair walking around downstairs.

"We can't get out with him down there," Jazz whispered.

"We might have to wait it out for a while."

"What will we do if he opens this closet to get a fresh towel or something?"

Phoenix didn't answer.

Neither of them wanted to imagine how Sinclair would react if he found the two of them holed up in his house.

As they waited, they realized they weren't going anywhere anytime soon. Sinclair made no move toward the stairs or the front door and so there was no way for Jazz and Phoenix to get out of the house undetected. Jazz had a moment to think how weird it was that this was the second time in two days she'd found herself squashed in a closet with Phoenix Lyons. They settled in as well as they could for a long, and uncomfortable, wait.

After a while, the space in the cupboard suddenly lit up as Phoenix reached for his phone and started scrolling through computing sites. He looked up at Jazz, face illuminated by his screen, and gave a shrug as if to say, *Well, what else are we going to do?*

Jazz reached into her pocket for her own phone, and started doing the same. As long as Sinclair stayed downstairs, they were safe enough.

Over the next couple of hours they listened as Sinclair shuffled about, doing the dishes, making a few phone calls. Jazz agonized at the thought of him going into the laundry to turn on the washing machine and noticing the broken door from the garage. Surely then he'd search the house and find them!

Jazz tried not to think too much about the time ticking away. They'd done so well to gather the fresh evidence in the first **48 HOURS** that led them to the perpetrator, but now that they'd found their suspect they were helpless to act!

Eventually they heard the noise they'd been dreading. Heavy footsteps came up the stairs, and walked across the landing, heading straight for the linen closet! Closer and closer they came. Jazz tried to shrink herself into the closet wall; she could feel Phoenix go rigid beside her. The footsteps paused and then continued until they heard a door opening and closing, and then silence.

Slowly, they exhaled. "He's gone into his bedroom," hissed Phoenix. "We have to take our chance." He dared to slide the closet door open a fraction and looked around, then turned back to signal to Jazz that the coast was clear. The two stepped quietly over to the staircase, grateful for the thick carpet that muffled the sound.

They finally reached the bottom of the stairs and Phoenix pointed to the back door. *This is too easy*, Jazz was thinking, hurrying after him when . . .

CREEAAAAK!

She stood on a creaking floorboard!

They heard the bedroom door opening upstairs and Sinclair came running down the stairs.

Phoenix reached the sliding doors at the back of the house and slid the heavy door across. "Quick! Hurry!" he hissed.

They hurtled outside, but found themselves on the manicured lawn with nowhere to hide and no escape route. "We'll have to go over the back fence. Come on!" Phoenix said as he took a running jump at the wooden fence. He hauled himself up, flinging first one leg, then the other over and jumping down to the other side. Jazz did the same, but as she scrambled to get her legs over the top of the fence, the back of her jacket caught on the fence post. She couldn't move.

"Hey, you up on the fence! What do you think you're doing busting into my house? You just wait till I catch you!" Cornelius Sinclair came barreling out of the house. Some of his muscle had turned to fat, and his hairline was now nonexistent rather than receding, but it was definitely the same man that they'd seen in the wedding portrait. Linda Sinclair's killer, within feet of them!

As Jazz desperately tried to free herself, Phoenix

reached back over the fence, yanked at her jacket and dragged her over. He caught her before she fell to the rough surface of the alley. Wordlessly, he took her hand as she scrambled to gain her balance and in seconds they were racing down the alley together.

A swift backward glance showed Sinclair's head peering over the fence. Jazz could see his pale face. But it was also clear that he was not going to be able to climb up and over. This didn't stop them running as fast as they could.

They ran until they could run no more, Phoenix pulling up, head to his knees, gasping for air. Jazz stopped beside him.

"That was a close call," he panted. Phoenix straightened up, hands on hips, breath starting to come more regularly. He glanced at Jazz, astonished to see a grin splitting her face from ear to ear.

He shook his head. "We almost get caught burgling the house of a known killer, and you look like you've just won the lottery. What gives?"

Excitement pulsed through Jazz. "We've got to get back to the Belmonts'. I know where the jewelry box is!"

09:00

There was no answer when they knocked on the Belmonts' front door. "How are we going to get inside?" Jazz wondered out loud.

"Just use your key," instructed Phoenix.

"Mmm. I'm not comfortable doing that when they're not here."

"You didn't mind using it before."

"That was different. That was when there was someone in the house."

"I don't get it. You don't mind walking in when someone is there, but you won't go in when no one's home!" He shook his head. "You don't make any sense!"

"It makes perfect sense!" retorted Jazz, her excitement replaced by anger. "Anyone else—anyone normal— would get it."

They glared at each other.

"So we're just going to wait until someone comes home?" Phoenix said. "We are up against the clock, remember. Sinclair said we have to return the jewelry box by midnight."

"You're right," she said. Finding Anika was far more important than worrying about getting in trouble with the Belmonts. It might feel odd, but she knew they were doing the right thing. It was like the saying Phoenix had quoted to her—fight with everything you've got. That's what they had to do to uncover the truth. She smirked as she fished out the key to Anika's house, thinking how unlikely it would have seemed two days ago that she'd be taking Phoenix Lyons' advice on anything. She had to admit though, they really were working on this as a team, and it obviously mattered to Phoenix that they saw it through.

Quietly, she unlocked the front door. With Phoenix close behind her, she stepped inside.

They made their way upstairs and then into Anika's room where Jazz closed the door with relief.

"Come on," said Jazz. "Let's see if I'm right."

"Hey, be careful!" he said. "You're about to tread on the squeaky floorboard."

"Help me shift the rug," she said. "The squeaky

floorboard is the clue!"

Phoenix got it straightaway. "It's loose! That's why it squeaks, right?"

Together they pushed back the bed and pulled out the rug, revealing the bare floorboards underneath.

"Look," pointed Jazz. "There are no nails fastening it down." She lifted the edge of the floorboard easily, while Phoenix shone his phone's flashlight into the small cavity underneath. Jazz reached in and felt around. Her hand touched something square and solid. She carefully lifted the box out of its hiding place. It was wooden and the initials LT could still faintly be seen, penciled on the top of the lid.

"Open it!" Phoenix whispered.

Cautiously, Jazz lifted the lid.

They peered into the interior. A stained envelope lay at the bottom of the box and written on it, in round handwriting, was the name "Linda Taylor."

Jazz froze.

"What are you waiting for? We have to see what's in it," urged Phoenix.

"But Sinclair's instructions were not to touch anything inside it. He said to just describe what could be seen in the box. If we open the envelope, he'll know, and Anika might . . ."

As Jazz tensed up, it seemed Phoenix's shoulders relaxed. "I know what to do," he reassured her. "He won't know that we've looked inside, I promise."

"You got a portable X-ray machine in your backpack?" Jazz said dryly.

Phoenix smirked. "Not quite. Like you said back at Sinclair's—let's go old school. Come on."

Clutching the jewelry box, Jazz followed Phoenix as they crept back down the staircase and into the kitchen.

Phoenix put the electric kettle on.

"You're making tea?" asked Jazz as she perched on a stool near the counter. "Milk with one sugar, thanks."

Phoenix ignored her as he stood by the kettle. When it was steaming, he took the jewelry box, opened it, and removed the envelope. Keeping his fingers at the very edge to avoid burning them, he moved the envelope backward and forward over the jet of steam. Within seconds the adhesive had softened. He removed the envelope from the steam, shaking it, cooling it down.

"Let me open it," said Jazz, putting her hand out to take it. "I'm the one who worked out where it was."

Reluctantly Phoenix handed the envelope over. "Be really careful," he warned. "It's got to look exactly the same as it did before."

Using only the most delicate pressure, Jazz peeled

the triangular fold of paper back from the main body of the envelope with her fingertips.

"What's in it?" Phoenix asked, peering inside as Jazz held the envelope open.

She looked closely too and then pulled back in disgust. "Yuck! How gross!"

Phoenix tore off a clean piece of paper towel from a roll on the wall, and delicately emptied the contents of the envelope onto it.

Together they stared at the grisly items.

"Nail clippings," said Jazz, grimacing. "And a lock of hair."

"With the right analysis, they'll prove how Linda Sinclair was murdered."

"You think they'll still hold traces of the poison?"

Phoenix nodded. "This is what she was talking about in the journal—what she was going to get her sister to hand over to the police. She must have become too weak before she got the chance. Maybe Neil found out and upped her dosage."

Jazz paced the kitchen as Phoenix pulled an evidence bag from his backpack and started tweezering in the nail clippings and hair.

"Phoenix, what are you doing?"

"What do you mean, what am I doing? This is what

we've been looking for—direct evidence."

"It's not that simple! Don't you see? This is also Anika's ticket home. We have to hand over the box so the Belmonts can tell Sinclair they have what he wants."

"And let him get away with it, with murder?!"

"Better than him murdering Anika!" Jazz cried.

Phoenix put the tweezers back on the counter. "Jazz," he said, his voice unexpectedly soft, "there's no guarantee that Sinclair will let her go. Just think about it. She is a key witness against him. If we take this evidence for analysis we will have something concrete for the police."

"But if he suspects . . ."

"He won't. Look, I'll probably only need a small amount of the sample. I'll put the rest back."

He returned most of the grisly items to the envelope which had contained them for over twenty years, pressing down the gummy seal again and replacing the whole thing back in the jewelry box.

The sound of car doors slamming startled them both.

"Anika's parents, they're back!" hissed Jazz.

They heard the front door open.

Phoenix pocketed his samples as Jazz stared guiltily at the kitchen door. What were the Belmonts going to think when they walked in and found them there?

07:55

Anika's parents came into the kitchen. Jazz saw the usually poised and elegant Mrs. Belmont looking disheveled and wretched. The anguish of the last day and a half was etched all over her face. She barely registered Jazz and Phoenix, and simply slumped onto a chair at the table.

"Jazmine!" said Mr. Belmont, sharply. "What are you doing here?"

Jazz picked up the box. "Mr. Belmont, Mrs. Belmont, we found the jewelry box." She held it out to them.

Mr. Belmont squinted. "Where did you find that?" His tone was far from friendly. "We tore the house to pieces and couldn't find anything."

"In Anika's room," Jazz stuttered. "We—"

"In Anika's room?" Mr. Belmont cut her off. "What

were you doing in there?"

"I, we—"

"My wife said you told her you knew nothing about the jewelry box! Why did you lie to us?"

"Oh, Mr. Belmont, please believe me! I didn't lie! All I knew then was that the kidnapper wanted some box I'd never even heard of!"

"What are you two up to?" demanded Mr. Belmont, the anger on his face mixed with grief and bewilderment. He suddenly noticed Phoenix, standing awkwardly in the corner of the kitchen. "And who are you?"

"This is Phoenix Lyons—"

Mr. Belmont cut her off. "Give me that box immediately!"

Jazz passed it to him but Mr. Belmont just seemed to get angrier. "Did you have something to do with my daughter's disappearance?" he demanded, glaring at Phoenix.

"Mr. Belmont," Jazz pleaded, "you're getting things all wrong! We're trying to help. Anika is my best friend in the world and Phoenix is helping me. Please listen to me. I can explain everything."

Mr. Belmont glared at both of them. "Has this whole thing been a setup—some sort of vicious prank? That's it, isn't it?"

"Stop blaming them, Harvey!" interrupted Mrs. Belmont. "They didn't do it. We need to tell the kidnapper that we have the box. Now!"

"Fine. I'll deal with you two later. For the moment, let's look in the box."

Phoenix and Jazz watched as Mr. and Mrs. Belmont opened the jewelry box and peered in. Jazz was relieved to see that the envelope looked exactly as it did when they'd found it.

"It's only an envelope with a name written on it," said Mrs. Belmont. "Is this what they want in exchange for my daughter?"

Her incredulous question went unanswered. Mr. Belmont pulled out his phone and clicked on the link to the blog the kidnapper had sent and started typing.

> BELMONT <

I've located the box. Inside is an envelope with the name Linda Taylor written on it. How do I get it to you? Is my daughter safe?

An anxious minute passed as they waited for a response.

> **> IDENTITY WITHHELD <**
>
> This is what you must do if you value your daughter's life. Go to Monash Park at 20:00 hours tonight. Place the box on the floor of the summerhouse in the middle of the park. Your daughter will be returned to you then. NO POLICE. Any police and the deal's off.
> You'll never see your daughter again.

"That's hours away!" cried Mrs. Belmont. "Oh, please, please let my darling Anika be OK."

"I'm sure everything will be fine now, Mrs. Belmont," Jazz said reassuringly. "You have what the kidnapper needs, there's no reason for them to hold Anika any longer."

She saw Phoenix giving her a look from across the kitchen that betrayed the concerns they'd shared just moments before. She tried to send "Be reassuring" vibes to him but instead he cleared his throat and said, "So, what's the plan for the drop-off?"

Mr. Belmont had been gripping the kitchen counter

for support, his head drooping, but now it snapped to attention.

"Plan? There's nothing to plan! I take the box to Monash Park, hand it over, and we get our precious girl back." He eyeballed first Phoenix and then Jazz and when he spoke again his voice was gruff. "Look, thank you for your help with the box, and I'm sorry about what I might have said or suggested—"

"It's OK, Mr. Belmont," Jazz interrupted. "We know you're under a lot of stress."

"Yes, we both are," he said, walking over and putting an arm around his wife. "We can resolve this tonight. However, we need you both to understand that this is a family matter. We will take care of it."

"Jazz, Phoenix, thank you for your help, but we'll take it from here," Mrs. Belmont added.

Both Jazz and Phoenix could read this as their cue to go.

"**W**hat if your mum's home?" asked Jazz, as they hurried toward Phoenix's house. "Will she let you into the lab?"

"Don't worry about her. I've got it covered," Phoenix said mysteriously, turning up the front walkway.

Phoenix bolted into his house, Jazz hot on his heels, the little packet of fingernails and hair tucked into his pocket.

"Mum!" he called. "Are you here?"

"I'm just on my way out," Dr. Lyons called, before coming into the living room. "Phoenix, what is it? Where have you been? You've done none of the chores we agreed. We're going to have to have a serious—"

She stopped herself as she noticed Jazz.

"Excuse me, I didn't realize you were here . . ."

She nodded at Jazz, but her eyes were on her son. "Phoenix?" she said, exasperation creeping back into her voice. "Are you going to introduce your friend? Don't tell me you've forgotten your manners as well as your responsibilities."

"Mum, this is Jazmine, I mean Jazz, but that's not important right now."

"Phoenix!" Dr. Lyons admonished.

"No, Mum, you don't understand. Jazz and me, we need your help. We need to get into the lab."

"Jazmine, it is a pleasure to meet you, but I'm afraid you must excuse us. I need to have a serious conversation with my son. Perhaps you'd like to help yourself to a drink from the kitchen?" Jazz took a step toward the door, keen to escape this awkward family scenario, but was stopped by Phoenix's yell.

"Mum! There's no time!"

"I would say time is exactly what you do have, Phoenix. You've had more than enough of it to write a letter of apology to your principal, which is what we agreed had to happen before you got any further work as my lab assistant."

Jazz tried to make herself as small as she could in the corner. She hadn't really believed Phoenix actually helped his mum for real.

"I've got it right here," Phoenix was saying, rummaging in his backpack. He pulled out a typed letter with his signature at the bottom.

His mum took it, her look of confusion deepening as she read through it.

"Phoenix, I don't understand. Your father and I have been asking you to do this since the day you were suspended."

"I was up late last night doing some . . . programming," Phoenix explained, winking at Jazz, "and I figured I may as well get it written. It says all the right things, doesn't it? Can I go in the lab now?"

Dr. Lyons waved a hand in the air. "It's beautifully written, Phoenix. I just wonder where this contrition suddenly came from."

"I did the wrong thing, I admit it. I was bored, OK? I'm good at computers, really good, and the stuff we do in class is just so easy. It was a challenge. Call it an extracurricular project."

"Hardly one I can see you getting extra credit for," remarked his mother, drily.

"I've got something way more interesting to do now, thanks to Jazz. But we need to get into the lab. Please, Mum?"

Dr. Lyons sighed. "I feel like there's more to this than

I can immediately understand, but I can't argue that you've kept your side of the deal. OK."

Phoenix grinned. "You're the best. Just one other thing—where do you keep the books on heavy metal spectrometry?"

* * *

Dr. Lyons had a work appointment, so after pointing Phoenix to the right resources, she left them in the lab.

"Ready to do some real science?" Phoenix said to Jazz. He leafed through the lab book that his mother had given him until he found the references to heavy metal tests. Following the instructions, he prepared the nail clippings and the hair.

First he rinsed them with acetone chloroform and deionized water, then carefully weighed half a gram each of the hair and nails, and placed the two samples in separate glass beakers. He then heated the samples on a hot plate and allowed them to cool.

"Now we can put them in the mass spectrometer," he said, satisfied.

Jazz looked at the machine he was indicating. It looked like a very large microwave oven, minus the front window. It had a printer and another unit attached to it.

"What does it do?" she asked.

"Basically you put either an electric or magnetic charge through whatever you're testing and the heat separates all the different components in the sample. It's kind of like trying to un-mix a cake after it's already been mixed up."

"Oh yeah, I think I've read about it," Jazz said. "Detectives can use it in arson investigations, to help figure out what started the fire."

"Sure, but true crime books normally only give you the end result. Watching how it happens? That's pure science." Phoenix gave a self-satisfied smile and flicked his hair.

What a show-off, thought Jazz.

Phoenix added an acid solution, then loaded the resulting samples into an autosampler cup. These went into the graphite furnace, and Phoenix waited for the automated process to do the rest. It was all very impressive and Jazz wondered if Phoenix might be trying to impress *her*.

"So what happens next?" Jazz asked.

"I've switched the machine on. You'll see the contents of the tube start to heat up and glow red. It will incinerate, releasing fumes that contain the elements in the nails and hair. Then the spectrometer program will analyze and identify the elements, matching them against a database of known minerals and chemicals until a result is found."

Jazz waited expectantly. But nothing happened.

Phoenix pressed the "Start Process" button again, frowning.

Once again, the samples remained exactly as he'd left them, in their small containers.

"They're not doing anything," Jazz said, giving him a hard look. "Is this a repeat of you and the DNA machine? Do you know what you're doing?"

"Of course I do! I've helped Mum prepare and load samples heaps of times."

"So why isn't it working?"

Phoenix tried to initiate the automated process one more time. To no avail. He could feel his face starting to go red.

"Hey, Einstein! Maybe you need me to help you!"

Phoenix turned around to see Jazz holding up the electric cord and plug.

"How about we plug it in? First rule: check power supply. It must have come out from the wall," she said, grinning.

She pushed the plug home and immediately the automated process began.

They watched the samples glowing through the glass window of the spectrometer.

"Once the samples have been all burned up, the computer program does its magic," said Phoenix, recovering his dignity as he explained. "The process doesn't take long. See! It's printing out already."

The printout was a graph of peaks and valleys. Phoenix scanned the results, ignoring the usual components found in fingernails like zinc, magnesium, chromium, calcium and other trace elements. His eyes were riveted on one word—a heavy mineral that shouldn't have been there and certainly not in such a high concentration.

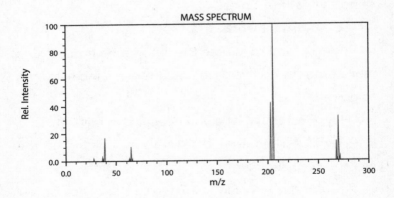

He stared at the word.

The mass spectrometer had found something bad in the nails and hair clippings. Something very bad indeed.

Phoenix looked up from the printout and met Jazz's

expectant gaze.

"Linda Sinclair was right to suspect her husband of murder," he breathed.

05:58

"Let me guess," said Jazz. "Arsenic?"

Phoenix shook his head. "That's what I'd thought too, as soon as I saw those nail and hair clippings. But there was no arsenic."

"What then?" asked Jazz. "The suspense is killing me!"

"Instead," he tapped a finger against the printout, "the mass spectrometer analysis shows very high—lethal—amounts of thallium."

"Thallium?" said Jazz. She flicked through Dr. Lyons' reference book until she found the right page and read out:

"Thallium is among the most serious toxicities. As it is odorless, tasteless and colorless it has been called 'the poisoner's poison' and also 'inheritance powder.' It is almost undetectable unless specific tests are carried out."

She looked up. "Sounds like pretty serious stuff."
Phoenix nodded.
Jazz kept reading.

"Symptoms of thallium poisoning include fever, gastrointestinal problems, racing heart, hallucinations and dementia."

Jazz sighed. "Poor Linda Sinclair," she said, "no wonder she thought she was going nuts. It was the poison all the time, affecting her brain!"

Jazz thought for a moment. "I know it was hard to detect, but wouldn't they have done a really thorough postmortem, since she died from some mystery illness? Wouldn't that have revealed the thallium?"

Phoenix shook his head. "She'd been under medical supervision—she talks about the doctor in her journal. He must have issued a death certificate and that was the end of it. There may not have been a postmortem at all."

"Remember in that last journal entry she said she'd been doing research? Linda must have found out about thallium as a possible method and was going to ask

Karen to arrange tests for it."

She took out her tablet and opened up CrimeSeen. She added in the new evidence.

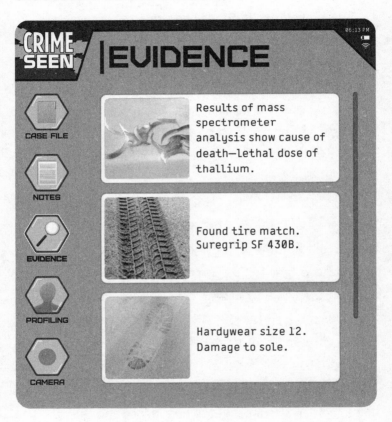

Jazz shuddered. It was one thing to read about a woman's suspicions that her husband was trying to murder her in a journal, but quite another to have those suspicions confirmed scientifically.

Phoenix gave Jazz a long look. "We have to go to the police."

Jazz opened her mouth to protest but Phoenix cut her off.

"This is the evidence we've been looking for! This, plus the journal being in Sinclair's house. Combined with everything else we've gathered, it's direct proof that the man's a murderer and kidnapper. We have to turn him in!"

"It's evidence we mostly gathered through trespassing and breaking and entering," countered Jazz. "Look, Phoenix, I agree this guy has to pay for what he's done, but, first of all, we need to make sure that Anika gets home safely."

Jazz looked at the time. It was **6:16 PM**. "There's less than two hours till the handover. Let's get out to Monash Park and make sure it all goes to plan. Then we'll know Anika's OK, we'll have her testimony, *and—*" she pointed at the nail and hair samples, "—we've still got some of the critical evidence. We know where Sinclair lives; it'll be easy enough to send the police to him."

Phoenix blew out a long breath.

"What about what Mr. Belmont said, to leave it to him to deal with the handover?" he asked.

"We can't let him go alone. He doesn't know what

he's up against. Sinclair has killed before, and Mr. Belmont may not be prepared for any tricks Neil has up his sleeve. Sinclair's clearly capable of being very dangerous! What if he wants to get rid of everyone who knows about the box—including Mr. Belmont? We have to see this through!"

Phoenix nodded slowly. "How are we going to get there?"

"Can you ask Simon again?"

"I'm sure I can convince him. I bet part of him is dying to know what we were really doing out in Sunshine Beach today." He reached for his phone.

"You're not going to tell him everything, are you?" said Jazz before Phoenix started dialing.

"Don't worry. I'll tell him just enough so he knows it's serious, but he doesn't need to know we're going to try to stop a murderer. You have to admit, a boxing coach like him would be good to have on our side in case things get messed up!"

04:27

Monash Park appeared as an eerie, dark landscape where the shapes of trees outlined against the night sky threw even darker shadows on the ground. Perimeter lights did little to brighten the gloomy few acres, even making the contrasting shadows seem blacker.

"Pull over up here," said Phoenix.

Simon brought the pickup to a stop in a dark spot near some trees. "I was almost scared to ask on the way," he said, shutting off the engine and lights. "But do you guys have a plan for helping your friend?"

"Of course," said Phoenix, sounding more confident than he felt. "It's like you always say: never go into a fight without a plan of attack."

"We'll be very careful," said Jazz in a low voice, vague enough not to alert Simon to the real seriousness of the circumstances.

"Look," said Phoenix, "someone's just pulled up near the big gates!"

"That's the Belmonts' car," said Jazz. "It's our cue to sneak into position, one of us on each side of the park."

"I'd better stay with the vehicle," said Simon, "in case you need a fast getaway."

Jazz looked at him, alert for any sign he was reading more into the situation, but she couldn't tell. He did seem very aware, so maybe Phoenix had let on more than he'd meant to about the kidnapping. In any case, Phoenix was right; it was good to know Simon was on their side.

Phoenix opened the car door and he and Jazz stepped out into the shadows.

Jazz wondered if Phoenix's heart was racing as hard as hers was—a mixture of excitement, anxiety and terror. She realized she was gripping her hands, blistered from her efforts to open the cellar cover, into tight, painful fists. She consciously made herself relax, taking in a deep breath. She needed to be calm and poised to deal with what might come next. For the moment, she forgot her stinging hands, aching muscles, and dry mouth. Everything came down to this. This was the exchange that would see her best friend returned to her from the clutches of a killer.

Beside her, Phoenix gave a determined nod. "OK. I'll take the western side of the park," he said, indicating the far edge of the park. "You take this side, Jazz. The minute you see anything, text me. I'll do the same."

Phoenix headed off through the darkness. He found a large tree with thick overhanging boughs and pressed himself flat against the trunk. From there, he could see the centrally positioned summerhouse, a circular building with open walls and a pitched roof, slightly raised above the ground. He waited.

Jazz hurried along the wrought iron fence that separated the park from the sidewalk next to the road. She thought she'd be feeling scared, being out in the night in a dark, cold park, but her powerful drive to rescue her friend overrode any such feelings.

She pushed her way into a tall hedge of shrubs that ran the length of the park's fence, letting parts of the foliage close around her. From where she crouched, she could see most of the summerhouse. She waited. She wondered where Mr. Belmont might be. Presumably he, too, was somewhere in the darkness, waiting . . .

Suddenly, the lights in the summerhouse went on. Puzzled, Jazz squinted to see what the light was revealing.

THE VANISHING

On the other side of the park, Phoenix peered around the tree to see what was happening.

A grotesque figure stood like an apparition in the center of the summerhouse, a gargantuan shape, lumpy limbs topped by an oversized, rounded head. Footsteps echoed across the park as Mr. Belmont hurried toward the summerhouse, a small, square object clutched in his hand. He, too, stopped and stared in astonishment at the giant figure.

Jazz blinked in disbelief. As her eyes adjusted to the light, she realized the monstrous figure was a person in a lab suit, the kind that people wore when they worked with highly contagious substances. Was it Neil Sinclair, hiding behind a disguise? The lighting made it impossible to be sure.

The figure moved, and Jazz could make out another inert shape. "Anika!" she gasped. The motionless figure of her best friend, head bowed, long brown hair streaming over her shoulders from under a beanie, was slumped on the floor of the summerhouse. Any moment now, she thought, her friend would be released. Anika would be free to go home to her family. Jazz watched Mr. Belmont place the jewelry box on the table in the center of the summerhouse, close to where the huge figure watched impassively from its masked eyes.

The silent night was shocked by a piercing sound from the road. A police siren! *What the . . . ! Why are the police here?* Jazz wondered.

Almost as quickly as it sounded, the siren cut out, but too late. Spooked, the kidnapper grabbed the jewelry box, and shoved Mr. Belmont roughly out of its way. He fell awkwardly and tumbled down the summerhouse steps as the suited figure ran from the park.

Jazz bolted toward the summerhouse, colliding full-on with Phoenix who was pelting after Anika's captor.

"He's getting away! We have to chase him!"

"The police can deal with Sinclair," Jazz said. "I have to get to Anika!" She pushed Phoenix aside and ran toward the summerhouse.

"Anika! Anika! It's OK! We're here to take you home! Everything is going to be all right!" she called out. There was no response. Anika did not lift her head.

"Anika?" she cried again as she reached her.

A dreadful fear clutched Jazz's heart. Her friend was so still, so silent. Sinclair couldn't have . . .

Phoenix ran past her as she hesitated, grabbing hold of Anika's shoulder, shaking her.

The beanie fell off and Phoenix lifted Anika's head.

But it wasn't Anika's head.

A painted, fixed smile and dead eyes met Jazz's own

shocked eyes—it was the wide, immobile face of what looked like a store mannequin.

Jazz felt rooted to the spot in shock and horror. She heard Mr. Belmont yell out in anguish, as he slumped on the stairs behind her. Somewhere, not too far away, she was aware of the sound of a car starting up.

"No!" Phoenix cried.

As Jazz put out her hand to touch the fake Anika, its body collapsed. "It's just empty coveralls!" she cried. Jazz turned to look at Phoenix, but was blinded by a flashlight shining in her face.

"Hold it right there. What do you two think you're doing in the park at this time of night? Read the signs. It closed hours ago!"

"Please, officer! You have to help us chase that person in the suit! Neil Sinclair!" Jazz cried. "It's not us you should be taking in!" But it was useless. The police officer had Phoenix by the shoulder. "You're trespassing. You're both coming with me now!"

Mr. Belmont, hobbling painfully, intervened. "It's OK. I'll handle these two. I can speak for them."

The officer released his hold and Mr. Belmont leaned in and whispered to Phoenix. "I can't chase the kidnapper." He gestured at his ankle, already swelling. "You have to catch them—go!"

Before the police officer knew what was happening, Phoenix and Jazz turned and ran as fast as they could.

"Simon might have seen the vehicle!" Jazz puffed. "We've got to try and follow it. Maybe it will lead us to Anika!"

They thudded along the path, using the lights from their phones to guide them through the darkness of the park. They raced across the road and flung themselves into Simon's truck.

"Did you just see a green SUV go past?" Jazz asked as she slid across the seat. Phoenix climbed in beside her.

"I sure did!" Simon replied.

"It was Sinclair! We need to get after him to help our friend. Go, go, go!" urged Phoenix.

"Ah, I thought you might say that," Simon said, quickly screeching away from the curb. He slid the pickup around in a U-turn, then accelerated in the direction taken by the kidnapper. "Whoever is driving that thing sure has a weird fashion sense."

When they came to the first crossroads Simon pulled up and said, "Which way?"

They could see no sign of the SUV in either direction.

"Time for eyes in the sky!" said Phoenix. He jumped from the car and pulled his drone out of his backpack.

It took a couple of minutes to set up, but as soon as its rotors were whirring Phoenix sent it up into the air, an image of all the surrounding streets now displayed on his phone screen. "There!" cried Phoenix, clambering back into the truck. "Go left!"

"Hurry up, Simon! We can't afford to lose him!" yelled Jazz.

Simon hurled his old pickup hard around a corner, causing Jazz to bump into Phoenix, who in turn bumped his head on the window, but they didn't care.

Jazz leaned forward, her body charged with energy and fear. They were getting closer to the place she might find her best friend.

The green SUV was some distance ahead of them, driving through an area largely deserted, apart from a few brightly lit showroom windows where displays ranged from bathroom fixtures to the occasional car showroom. In the distance, they heard a train, its rhythmic rattling the only sound apart from the pickup's engine. Beside her, Phoenix kept his eyes glued to the drone footage as the device tracked the SUV, and directed Simon at each turn.

"He's slowing down," Phoenix reported, "and turning off the road. Hang back, Simon, we don't want him to know we're here."

They pulled up well behind the green SUV. As they watched, the car drove into the driveway of a large industrial building surrounded by a chain-link fence. Simon waited a few moments before edging slowly down the road and past the entrance. Craning their necks, they saw Sinclair's car had stopped in a dimly lit parking space to the side of the factory complex. A suited figure was disappearing into the front door of the building, over which glowed a sign announcing the business as PathTech Lab Solutions.

"Anika is in there, I know it," said Jazz. "We have to find her." She checked the time on her phone: **9:30 PM**. It had been almost **48 HOURS** since Anika had been taken. A horrifying thought occurred to her, and she turned to Phoenix.

"What if Sinclair has come back to get rid of Anika, now that he thinks we've called the police? He knows we've been at his house, and must suspect we have evidence that could incriminate him."

"We've got to get in there, now," Phoenix said, landing the drone and reaching for the door handle.

"Hang on just a sec," said Simon, grabbing Jazz's arm. "What have you two gotten yourselves into?"

"We have to save my friend," replied Jazz.

"Call the police," Phoenix instructed Simon. "Tell

them where we are. Then stay with the truck."

Simon went to argue, but Phoenix surprised them all and looked at him imploringly. "Please!" he begged. "We might need to leave in a hurry."

02:15

At the door to the lab, Jazz turned the handle. "It's not locked," she hissed at Phoenix, stepping inside. As their eyes became accustomed to the dark, they saw a reception area to their left and a curtained-off area to their right. In between, a dimly lit corridor stretched ahead of them.

"Careful," whispered Phoenix. "We mustn't alert him."

"We should check behind those curtains," said Jazz.

"The drone isn't the only thing that can see in the dark," said Phoenix. He pulled out his phone and attached a device over the lens. Switching to camera mode, the screen at first showed nothing but blackness, then suddenly a full picture emerged.

"Infrared on the phone," whispered Jazz. "Nice."

They both gasped in surprise when Phoenix aimed

the phone at the curtains. Behind the long drapes, the image showed dozens of strange shapes.

"What is all that?" Phoenix whispered. "Nothing's moving. What are they?"

Jazz crept forward to where the curtains hung on their head-high rails. She pulled the end curtain open.

Phoenix jumped back instinctively.

"What the—?" Jazz's shocked voice faltered.

For one horrifying instant, Phoenix and Jazz thought they were looking at a whole lot of ghostly corpses hanging on racks, but as their eyes adjusted to the display, they realized that they were looking at lab suits, much like the ones they'd borrowed from Dr. Lyons' lab to investigate Anika's room. Hanging here in the dim light of a deserted lab, with a killer lurking nearby, they had looked far more threatening.

"Come on," Jazz said, tugging Phoenix's arm, "we have to find Anika!"

Keeping low, the two of them scurried down the corridor to the other end, where some light showed. They paused at a glass-windowed door, but when they peeked through, they could see only a darkened hallway with another door at the end of it and many more closed doors on either side.

They went in and hurried along the hallway, opening

doors and calling Anika's name in desperate whispers. "Anika! Anika? Are you in here?"

"What if she's been drugged and can't speak?" Jazz whispered as they came to the last two doors on either side of the corridor. They looked in each one, stepping inside, checking thoroughly. Nothing. One was being used for storage and filled with boxes, the other an office with folders on the shelves.

Another door stood closed at the end of the hallway. Jazz reached out for the handle.

"Wait," hissed Phoenix. "Sinclair isn't in any of these other rooms. We don't know where he is. What if he's on the other side of this door?"

"What if Anika is?" Jazz hissed back. She turned the handle slowly. Ahead of them was a large hangar-like space, being used as a garage. Several cars marked with "Urgent blood delivery" stood parked beside a stack of wood pallets.

Jazz shivered. Sinclair could be crouched down in the darkness, just waiting to pounce on them.

"I'm going to search the vehicles," she whispered to Phoenix. "You keep an eye out for Sinclair." With a racing heart and almost too tense to breathe, she ran on tiptoe from car to car, softly calling her best friend's name, silently peering through the windows while

Phoenix kept a lookout by the door. No sign of Anika. She stopped after checking the last of the cars. The sudden silence felt menacing, as if they were waiting for something terrible to happen. Jazz felt goose bumps rising. Had they walked right into a trap?

"Maybe Anika isn't even here. Maybe Anika is—" Jazz jumped as Phoenix put his hand on her arm.

"Did you hear that?" he hissed.

Jazz listened but all she could hear was the blood pounding in her ears. She took some deep breaths to calm herself. Finally, she breathed a little easier. "I can hear something. It seems to be coming from that corner over there," she said, pointing.

Phoenix leaned forward. "There it is again!"

She grabbed Phoenix's arm. "This is the place! Anika is here!"

Phoenix picked up a heavy monkey wrench and Jazz found a pair of bolt cutters that she thought would make a good club. Armed with these, they tiptoed across to the corner where the noise came from. They discovered a small door set into the wall. Closer they crept, until they could see that the door was closed with two shiny, new heavy-duty bolt slide locks.

Jazz felt excitement stirring, helping her forget her fear and exhaustion.

Phoenix said in a low voice, "We know Sinclair isn't in there—not with those locks in place on the door. But if he shows up, we've got to be ready to take him down. I'll hit him first and if that doesn't work, you're my backup. OK?"

Jazz nodded. "OK. But I kind of wish Simon had come inside with us now."

"Me too," Phoenix admitted.

Jazz gripped the bolt cutters tightly, holding her breath, as Phoenix opened the first bolt lock and then the second.

01:35

Carefully, silently, Jazz turned the handle and swung the door open. Inside was a tiny bathroom, just a toilet and sink, that seemed to be given over to storing cleaners' supplies. There were mops and buckets stacked against the maze of plumbing pipes. Among them, eyes full of fear, crouched Anika.

"Anika!" Jazz said as softly as she could.

The fear changed to tears of joy.

"Anika! You're alive!" said Jazz, darting over to her.

"Jazz? It's really you!" cried Anika. Then she saw who Jazz was with. "Phoenix? Phoenix *Lyons*? What are you doing here?" Phoenix grinned and shrugged.

"We'll fill you in later," said Jazz to Anika. "Let's get you out of here first."

"I'll need some help with that," Anika said as she raised

her arm to show them a long heavy chain padlocked around her.

Jazz opened the bolt cutters wide and slowly cut through the chain.

Finally, Anika staggered to her feet. "I thought no one would ever find me!" she cried, throwing her arms around Jazz and Phoenix, who in turn threw his arms around the pair of them in a group hug. "Thank you, thank you! You saved me! I never thought anyone would come!"

"*Now*, let's get you out of here," said Jazz.

They started hurrying across the garage floor, eyes peeled for any sight of Sinclair.

"Have you seen who kidnapped me? Do you know who it is?" Anika asked. "They're wearing some weird suit. I've never seen their face."

"Anika, you're not going to believe this. The kidnapper is Neil Sinclair!" Seeing the blank look on Anika's face, Jazz went on as they neared the entrance to the long corridor. "The LT in your journal, her maiden name was Linda Taylor. She was married to Neil Sinclair and he's the one who murdered her!"

"What?!" said Anika. "But how—"

"Sorry to interrupt, but can we save the debrief for when we're out of here?" Phoenix said. "Come on!"

Jazz grabbed hold of Anika's hand tightly, leading her to the corridor. Almost immediately the sound of footsteps stopped them in their tracks.

"Someone's coming!" Anika whispered.

Phoenix froze, listening.

An icy fear ran through Jazz's body. "Quick! It must be Sinclair! He's coming this way!"

"Get ready to take him down! Remember what I said, Jazz. I'll whack him as soon as he comes through the door. You're my backup!"

Jazz tightened her grip on the bolt cutters and the three of them pressed themselves against the wall next to the doorway to the corridor, Jazz and Anika on one side, Phoenix on the other with the monkey wrench raised high. A stout man with a bald head appeared in the doorway. Sinclair! Phoenix raised the monkey wrench and brought it down hard, catching Sinclair on the shoulder. He sprawled forward, yelling in pain and surprise. Jazz and Anika fell on top of him, pinning him to the floor.

"I'll give you another whack," Jazz threatened, waving the bolt cutters around, "if you dare move!"

Stunned, Sinclair stopped struggling. "What do you want?" he roared. "If it's money, there's none here! Hey! You're the criminals who broke into my house!"

"*You're* the criminal!" Jazz roared. "You're a kidnapper! A murderer!"

"What are you talking about? What are you doing here? I'll call the police!"

"We've already done that for you," sneered Phoenix. "Come on, Sinclair, we know that you murdered your wife! This is the end for you!" Phoenix threw himself down and sat on Sinclair's back with Jazz and Anika keeping the man's shoulders and arms pinned to the floor.

"Get off me, you little thugs! I don't know what you're talking about. My wife died after a long illness! How dare you say that I murdered her?"

"A long illness that you created!" Jazz said. "We've read the journal. You had to get your hands on the jewelry box because that's where Linda had left the evidence of you poisoning her! But you didn't know that we'd already helped ourselves to a sample!"

"I have no idea what you're talking about!" Sinclair screamed.

"Oh yeah?" said Phoenix. "What are you doing here so late at night?"

"Something set off the alarm; I got an alert at home."

"Don't try to play innocent with us. We know all about the toxin. We even have the proof now. Linda passed it to us from beyond the grave," Jazz said.

"Toxin? Linda? Proof? You're out of your minds!" Sinclair raged.

"You're the crazy one who climbed into my room in the middle of the night and kidnapped me!" cried Anika. "And now I'm hearing you were the one who killed the woman in the journal. With poison! I've been chained up in a tiny room by a murderer for two days!"

"Kidnapper? Chained? Murderer? You kids are nuts," yelled the struggling man. "You've been watching too much television. Let me go!"

"I don't think so," said Jazz. "The only place you're going is jail."

A sound in the corridor made them all look up. Even Sinclair stopped struggling. Jazz, Phoenix and Anika went still, exchanging looks of terror.

Some *thing* had appeared in the doorway.

00:59

"What the—?" Phoenix's startled voice broke the silence.

Filling the doorway was a figure in a white suit, looking like a spaceman, landed from Mars. In the darkened lab the hood covering its head was a blank mask.

This couldn't be happening—but it was!

This was the figure that had fled from Monash Park when the hostage exchange went wrong. But it was even more terrifying. In the figure's right hand was a gun. And it was pointed straight at them!

"Marvelous!" hissed the voice behind the mask. "All my problems in one place. Now I can deal with you all at once."

For a split second, no one moved . . .

Then came an explosion of action.

Phoenix, using the fighting skills that Simon had taught him, charged full tilt.

"Oof!" came a gasp as his opponent staggered backward.

Jazz stood up and swung the bolt cutters, bashing the arm holding the gun as hard as she could with the heavy tool. The gun flew out of the rubbery hand that had grasped it as the figure toppled forward.

Neil Sinclair got to his feet, knocking Anika aside, and jumped on top of the suited figure as it fell face-first to the ground. "Who are you?" he roared.

Phoenix reached for the mask and yanked it off.

Sinclair gaped in shock and let go as the person rolled onto their back. Peering up at them was a woman's pale face. She had brown eyes and strands of curly dark hair sticking out around her head.

Neil blinked. "Karen?"

"Karen?" repeated Jazz. "As in Karen Taylor, Linda's helpful sister?"

Phoenix, Anika and Jazz gazed at the woman lying on the floor, whose face crumpled with rage and frustration. "Let me go!" she yelled. The menace had left her voice now that it was no longer modulated through the breathing apparatus in the oversized hood of the lab suit.

"Not until you explain yourself!" Sinclair demanded. He rose slowly to his feet, and rubbed at his shoulder where Phoenix had landed the blow with the monkey wrench.

"Could someone please tell me . . . what is going on?" Sinclair was roaring no more, a look of pure bewilderment coming over his face as he stared down at his sister-in-law.

"It's all a mistake. You have to trust me," Karen blurted.

"I'm not so sure about that. It was surprising enough when you turned up at the house 'on vacation' the other day, Karen, but now, showing up here, with a gun? And who are these kids?"

"These little meddlers are trying to come between us! They're trying to spoil everything!" cried Karen. "Don't listen to them!"

"I'm afraid you do need to listen to us, Mr. Sinclair," said Jazz.

"Karen used thallium to poison your wife," said Phoenix.

The woman raised herself to a sitting position.

"They're lying! Monstrous lies, Neil!" she screamed. "They're troublemakers. I came here to help you deal with them!"

"Thallium?" Sinclair said, his eyes wide. "Thallium?"

"It's all lies!" Karen screeched, sounding unhinged.

"You're a scientist," said Phoenix to Sinclair. "You must know it's the perfect poison. You know it fits with your wife's symptoms. Think about it."

Neil Sinclair stared at his sister-in-law, the bewilderment on his face turning to deep shock as he worked through what Jazz and Phoenix had told him.

Sinclair's face went white as the realization hit him. "You murdered Linda?" His eyes blazed with rage toward Karen.

"It's a lie!" she said desperately.

"You did! That's why we could never work out what was wrong with her. You killed my beautiful wife!"

He grabbed the gun from the floor, aiming at a spot on Karen's forehead. His hands were shaking but his voice was steady. "Tell me the truth, Karen."

Karen slumped back down to the floor, hands crossed in front of her face. "Don't shoot me! I'll tell you! I'll tell you everything!" She raised herself to her feet. Neil's aim didn't waver. Karen's voice was calm now as she began to speak.

"You know the boy's right, Neil, thallium is the perfect poison. It started with those care packages I used to send Linda—trace amounts injected into Cherry de Lix chocolates. I knew I had to be there to make sure she was dosed up enough so that the end would come. That's why I came to stay with you. But then Linda started to suspect something. Maybe she'd learned something about poisons, spending all those years around pathologists. She told me she had evidence hidden away somewhere. So I upped the dosage. She died before she could do anything with it. I looked but never located the evidence, so I thought maybe she'd made it up. Anyway, the secret died with her. Until this one—" Karen turned her narrowed eyes at Anika, "—found that journal. I didn't know Linda had written everything down."

"Journal? What journal?" Sinclair's voice was barely a whisper.

"I found it in my room, behind an antique mirror," explained Anika. "A journal written by a woman who had lived in that very room twenty years earlier. She suspected her husband of murdering her."

"Me?" Now Sinclair's voice rose in a shrill cry. "She suspected me? Karen, how could you do this? Why did you do this? She was your own sister!"

"I did it for you, Neil!"

"For me?" Neil looked horrified.

"Yes. So I could be with you. You should have married

me! I was the clever one. I was much prettier than Linda. I understood about your work. I was the obvious choice. I did what I had to do, and then I waited for you."

The two adults seemed oblivious now to the three teenagers who stood by, watching them, agog.

"What are you talking about?" Neil whimpered.

"I could hear it in your voice, when we used to talk while Linda was sick. You sounded so sad, frustrated. I'd tell you about all the fun things I was doing and I'd hear you becoming so wistful. I was trying to tell you—that wonderful life you'd been having with Linda could still happen, could happen with me, when we were finally together."

"Us, together?" Sinclair looked at Karen with a face of pure disgust. "Is . . . is that why you kept calling me after she died? I was grieving."

Karen's calm voice suddenly rose to a shriek again. "You still didn't turn to me. Instead you just sold up and disappeared! You didn't even tell me where you were."

"You were pressuring me," Neil said. "I didn't want you around once Linda died."

"But you were free!"

"You 'freed' me from Linda? By murdering her? I couldn't love anyone other than Linda, certainly not her murderer! How did you think you could get away with such a thing?"

"I have! For twenty years!" shrieked Karen. "And I didn't just come here for a vacation, Cornelius," spat Karen. "I had to take care of this kid who was threatening to spill everything all over the internet."

"How did you find my blog?" asked Anika.

"I've had a search alert set up for 'Deepwater,' just to keep an eye on what was happening in the neighborhood. Remember that ghost story you wrote, set in that 'spooky old mansion'? The one talking about spying on the house next door? You stupid girl, you gave me the idea!"

Anika's eyes widened in horror.

"That's right, this is all your fault. You're the one who wrote the story, found the journal and decided to blog it all! I knew you had to be stopped." Karen looked at Anika with pure venom in her eyes.

"So hang on, this is all because I blogged that journal?" said Anika. She shivered.

Karen ignored Anika and turned her evil gaze to Neil. "And you. I knew I'd be able to borrow your car, find a lab suit, even wear your work boots. Getting into Anika's house was easy—I knew all about the old laundry chute. It all went perfectly, until these kids got involved and ruined everything!"

Neil Sinclair loosened his hold on the gun and it slid

to the floor.

Karen's rage now boiled over. "I even came back to give you a second chance and you still rejected me!" she screamed, standing up and starting to walk menacingly toward Neil.

"You're not going anywhere," said Jazz as Phoenix pushed the struggling woman back down while Jazz quickly tied the laces of the Hardywear boots together. Now, if Karen Taylor tried to run, she'd fall flat on her face.

Just then, Simon ran in yelling, "The cops are almost here!"

"I can hear the sirens!" Phoenix agreed.

But it was too late. Karen, seeing her plans falling apart, had taken advantage of the momentary distraction provided by Simon's arrival, and had torn the boots off and was already halfway down the corridor, grabbing the gun on the way. She ran out the door.

"After her!" Phoenix yelled. "Quick! She's getting away!"

Everyone raced after Karen. Phoenix and Simon were the fastest. They reached the door first and flung it open, then sprinted outside. As they got out into the cold night air, they saw Karen pelting through the parking lot. They chased her but in no time she was at the road. They saw her risk a quick look back at her pursuers. Simon and Phoenix were gaining on her, with Anika, Jazz and Neil behind them. Karen turned back around and suddenly swerved to the side of the road—where Simon's pickup was parked.

"Stop! Don't you dare!" yelled Simon. He turned to Phoenix and said, "She's stealing my truck! And I've gone and made it easy for her—I left the keys in there. She's really going to pay for this."

The engine throbbed as it started and the truck sped off. Simon kept running after it, yelling in desperation. The pickup headed into a bend in the road so fast that it teetered briefly on two wheels. There was no way he'd catch it. Simon stopped in the middle of the road.

"Come on," panted Neil, as everyone caught up with Simon. "Quickly, let's go get my car. We can't let her get away."

"No, you go. I'm going to stay here and wait for the cops," said Simon, tugging his ginger hair in anger. "She's not going to get away with this."

Phoenix awkwardly patted his coach on the back, and then quickly followed Neil as he led everyone else back toward the lab building, then around to the side where his car was parked. They all piled into his green SUV.

Sinclair took off so fast that the back door swung wide open. Jazz precariously leaned out, grabbed the handle and slammed the door shut.

Sinclair accelerated, pushing them all against their seats. They tore out of the parking lot, turning with a squeal onto the main road.

"I always knew there was something wrong with Karen," said Sinclair, his eyes never leaving the road. "She was so . . . well, self-centered doesn't cover it."

"Narcissist," said Jazz.

"What?" he said sharply, snapping his head to glance at her before returning his intent gaze to the truck in front of them.

"That's what she called Anika on her blog. It's someone with an exaggerated idea of their own importance and achievements."

Neil Sinclair nodded grimly. "That sounds about right."

"Narcissists often project their issues onto others. She was the one putting those nasty comments on your blog, Anika, both to discredit you and to try to scare you off. You were getting too close to the truth. She wanted to make it look like you were just showing off, when really you were solving an important crime."

Anika reached across and gave Jazz's hand a squeeze.

Jazz smiled in return, knowing their fight about the journal was over.

"It's also why she was going on about being prettier and smarter than—" Jazz faltered for a moment, before finishing, "—than your wife."

A tear ran down Neil Sinclair's face. "It was only ever Linda that I loved. After she died I couldn't be near anyone who'd known her. I couldn't bear even being in that house!" he broke off, and gulped. "I sold it, the location of some of our happiest moments. Memories. I moved to the beach and set up this business. I never forgot her, never married again either, but things had gone back to a sort of normal. Until now."

Grim determination set in again on Sinclair's face. The car responded with a roar as he urged it on in pursuit.

The truck was dashing toward a railroad crossing. Its red lights started flashing and they heard the ding-dong of its warning signal.

"If she gets across and we're held up by the train, we could lose her!" said Jazz.

"We can't let her escape!" Anika added.

In the distance, the faint rumble of a train became louder. Behind them, they heard the wailing sirens of approaching police cars.

Phoenix groaned. "She's going to get through before the cops make it here! She's getting away!"

"The cops won't know where to go!" Jazz cried.

Sinclair stepped on the gas even harder and his powerful vehicle surged after the truck. To his right, Phoenix could see the lights of the speeding train getting much closer, while ahead of them, Karen also gunned the motor.

"Stop!" yelled Phoenix.

Cornelius slammed on the brakes. "She's insane! She'll never make it!"

As they jolted to a stop, they watched with increasing horror as Karen raced toward the railroad crossing, the train sprinting along its rails heading for the same spot. Suddenly they heard the scrape of brakes as the engineer saw the vehicle flash onto the tracks. The train screamed as it tried to stop in time.

But it was too late.

In a violent collision, Simon's pickup and the train created the point of a perfect—and perfectly lethal—right angle. A deafening bang caused them all to jump in shock as the truck was obliterated.

Phoenix, Jazz and Anika jumped out of Sinclair's car, running toward the railroad crossing as finally the last of the train's carriages came to a halt.

They stared down the embankment on the left of the crossing at what was left of Simon's pickup. The train had hit the vehicle right on the driver's door, which was now squashed as close to the passenger side as two pieces of sliced bread.

No one could have survived the impact.

There was no hope at all for Karen Taylor.

00:0

0:00

CASE SOLVED

Light and noise erupted around the scene. Police cars and ambulances screeched to the spot. Their sirens were soon drowned out by the persistent stutter of a police helicopter overhead, its glaring spotlight dulling the red-and-blue strobing of the emergency vehicles.

As shaken passengers were herded off the train, ambulance workers checked them over. Once cleared of injury, they crowded around the embankment looking at the wreckage. The shocked engineer, head in hands, spoke to the police.

Simon had arrived in a police car, and he was speaking to the cops as well, along with a distraught Neil Sinclair.

Jazz, Anika and Phoenix stood in a huddle. Worry furrowed their brows until eventually it became clear that no one from the train was seriously injured. There were just a few bruises and sprains.

Soon enough there would be reporters and news cameras hovering around, but for now, there was a sense that the chaos was easing. And not just for the passengers.

Jazz, Phoenix and Anika started to relax. Still the trio stood in silence, unsure where to start. There was so much to fill each other in on. So much had happened in the past **48 HOURS**. They would be forever changed.

Anika broke the silence. "I was so frightened. I had no idea where I was. Karen must have drugged me. I remember being in my bedroom with an intruder, then there was a pain in my neck and then I woke up in that tiny room and couldn't get out. It was horrible. Whenever Karen showed up to give me some food she was always in that freaky costume. I had no idea she was even a she! Or worse, what she was going to do with me." Anika shuddered.

"You're safe now," Jazz said, a reassuring arm around her best friend's shoulders. "We have to tell Mack!" she exclaimed. She held her phone at arm's length and snapped a picture of the two of them, excitedly tapping out the message, "We did it!" before sending it on to their friend.

Anika gave a shake of her head, still trying to convince

herself she was really free. "There's one thing you have to tell me, where was the jewelry box?"

"It was in your room all along! You won't believe what I was doing when I worked out where it was hidden."

"You mean what *we* were doing," interrupted Phoenix. "We solved this as a team, remember?"

"That's another thing you'll have to fill me in on!" smiled Anika. "Thank goodness Linda never gave that box to Karen, or told her what was in it. She would have destroyed it for sure. Then, even if I'd still found the journal, we would never have been able to find out the truth."

An unmarked police car pulled up. "It's Mum and Dad!" Anika cried, running into her mother's arms. Mr. Belmont waited his turn and then the three of them hugged each other, laughing and crying together.

Jazz stood by, watching the joyous family reunion, her hair blowing crazily in the down draft from the helicopter. She felt so proud that she and Phoenix had helped to bring Anika to this moment of safety and love.

Mrs. Belmont went over to Jazz and hugged her, too. "Thank you, thank you, Jazz. I thought I would never see my beautiful daughter ever again." Her voice faded away.

"You don't have to thank me, Mrs. Belmont. It's what

best friends do." She winked at Anika, who grinned back at her.

Once the police scheduled appointments for the Belmonts, Sinclair, Simon, Jazz and Phoenix to give their statements the next day, Jazz glanced at her watch. It was after midnight. The **48 HOURS** after Anika had been kidnapped had passed. And they'd done it—not only had they gathered all the evidence they needed to identify the kidnapper and solve a cold case, but they'd also found and rescued her friend.

"I just wanted to thank you kids," said Neil as he prepared to leave. "It has all been a terrible shock. My wife's own sister killed her? And now she's gone and I can't . . ." He paused. "It . . . it breaks my heart to think that Linda believed I was trying to get rid of her."

"I'm so sorry, Mr. Sinclair. It's a lot to take in. And we're sorry we broke into your house as well. Sorry we suspected you of something so awful."

Sinclair nodded that he understood, then held his hand out to shake, first to Jazz then Phoenix. "I know you were trying to save your friend."

"When you get the chance, I think you should read Linda's journal. Karen hid it at your house," Jazz said.

Neil shook his head.

"I don't think I could. It would be . . . too painful."

Jazz nodded. "I understand," she said gently. "I think the last entry might help, though. Linda wrote, 'How could I have been so wrong about the man I married?'" Jazz looked up into Neil Sinclair's face, and placed a hand on his arm. "I believe that entry means she knew, Mr. Sinclair. She knew it wasn't you."

It was Sinclair's turn to nod. He was struggling to hold back tears. "That makes me feel a little better. Thank you."

They said good night to Anika and left her safely in the company of her relieved parents.

* * *

Jazz, Phoenix and Simon got a lift home in the back of a police car. Jazz could see Phoenix was shaken up by the whole incident, and she put her hand over his and gave it a gentle pat as they traveled on in silence.

"I honestly didn't think we'd be able to save her," she admitted. "But we did it."

Phoenix smiled.

The first stop was Schmick n Fit. As Simon got out of the police car, Jazz climbed out too and threw her arms around him with Phoenix close behind her. "We couldn't have done it without you, Simon. Thank you so much for everything . . . and I'm so sorry about your truck."

"Me too," said Phoenix, shaking his hand. "Really sorry."

"Not as sorry as I am," said Simon.

"If it helps I'll service the next one you get for free," said Phoenix. "I'm not just a brilliant mind—I have mechanical skills as well."

"A bit of humility and you'll have the whole package," teased Jazz.

The next stop was Jazz's place, where her mother and Tim were waiting for her. It was clear from her mother's face that any trouble she might have been in for getting mixed up in the investigation of a kidnapping murderer over the last two days, and lying about it, had been set aside, for now. Jazz clambered out of the police car and hugged her mother. She turned back and saw Phoenix standing awkwardly by the side of the vehicle. She walked up to him, unsure how to say goodbye.

"I guess this is it," said Jazz. She stuck her hand out to shake his, but found herself pulled into a hug instead.

They gripped each other tightly for a moment, but just as quickly it was over. They both shuffled their feet and stared at the ground.

"Hey, so, Phoenix," Jazz started. "You want to hang out in the lab again sometime?"

"Are you asking me out?" he said.

The look on his face made her burst out laughing. "Very funny! I was thinking we could do some more lab work! Maybe your mum needs another assistant?"

"I think that can be arranged," said Phoenix with a grin.

"So I'll see you back at school?"

"Good chance."

Phoenix got back into the police car and gave the driver his address. As the car pulled away, the police officer sitting beside the driver turned and said, "You'll sure have a story to tell the kids at school, won't you, pal?"

"School," said Phoenix, shaking his head. "It's been a while. You know . . . I'm actually looking forward to it."

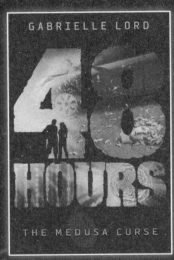